CHOOSE YOUR OWN

LOVE STORY

CHOOSE YOUR OWN

LOVE STORY

(MIS)ADVENTURES IN LOVE, LUST,
AND HAPPY ENDINGS

ILYSE MIMOUN

RUNNING PRESS
PHILADELPHIA · LONDON

Published by Running Press,
A Member of the Perseus Books Group

Printed in China

Books published by Running Press are available at special discounts for bulk pur-
chases in the United States by corporations, institutions, and other organizations.
For more information, please contact the Special Markets Department at the
Perseus Books Group, 2300 Chestnut Street, Suite 200, Philadelphia, PA 19103, or
call (800) 810-4145, ext. 5000, or e-mail special.markets@perseusbooks.com.

ISBN 978-0-7624-5851-6

Library of Congress Control Number: 2015934575

E-book ISBN 978-0-7624-5852-3

9 8 7 6 5 4 3 2 1
Digit on the right indicates the number of this printing

Design by Josh McDonnell
Edited by Jordana Tusman
Typography: Bembo and Brandon

Running Press Book Publishers
2300 Chestnut Street
Philadelphia, PA 19103-4371

Visit us on the web!
www.runningpress.com

Once upon a time you were in love with a guy named Greg.

But, oh no! Greg dumps you for a girl with amazing thighs and zero personality.

You are forced to suffer online dating, scrolling through dudes with big egos and small vocabularies.

Until, behold! You meet a sexy, charming guy named Jun . . .

. . . But is he charming like a prince? Or charming like a player?

How will your story end? Are you ready to find out?

IF YOU'RE READY to start your own romantic adventure, begin on page 6. A world of decisions sits before you on the following pages, and you alone are in charge of what happens. Some of your choices will be amazing. Some will suck. Don't worry—you can always go back and start again! You don't get that option in real life, so go ahead and savor it. Oh, and this isn't the kind of book that you read straight through—just follow along and see where the story takes you by making a new choice at the end of each section. (You can also turn down the corner of the page each time you make a decision; that way, you can return to the page and make a different choice.)

Of course, dating is not for the thin-skinned. Broken hearts and annoying advice from married friends may await you. But maybe—just maybe—you'll find your happily ever after. . . . Good luck!

1

It's a muggy Sunday in September and you have just been dumped.

Greg is leaving you for a little sylph named Oasis, and that is not a joke. *Her name is Oasis.* He met her at Burning Man. Oasis is a goddamn whimsical free spirit, or what Burners call a "sparkle pony." She flutters and flits and giggles and gurgles because she is an infant, and apparently that is what Greg likes.

But why would Greg like that? Good question! The answer is that Oasis is hot. She has long tan legs, mermaid hair, and a wide mouth like Vivian in *Pretty Woman*—a character (you are fond of pointing out) whose evolution from "sassy sex object" to "classy sex object" is not exactly empowering. Until recently Greg liked this sort of cultural criticism, but Oasis has the legs and the hair and the mouth. You have legs and hair and a mouth, but your legs are pale, your hair is frizzy, and your mouth is just okay. Not assets. So that's one thing.

Greg also likes Oasis because she's fun. She likes clubbing, she likes smoking a bowl with the guys, and she likes night swimming at the beach because she has the body and is not afraid of sharks. She is also what your Grandma would have called a "courva." That's Yiddish for slutty. All those things are fun for boys.

You like staying in, ordering Thai food, and watching television.

You love food so much, in fact, that you're a food critic for a living. The money is terrible, but you get to eat a lot of weird and delicious ethnic noodles. In fact, you and Greg used to eat pad thai noodles together and make fun of girls like Oasis—girls who wear Playboy pendants and think that yoga pants make you spiritual.

Maybe he loves her because she's simply happy and free instead of anxious and insecure—like you. You think too much. You worry. You care. You probably worry and care too much, but you were hoping that was part of your charm. It's awful to consider that the very thing that makes you *you* might have sent your boyfriend running for the hills.

After all, just a few weeks ago you stayed up all night discussing whether happiness was a realistic goal or if it just sets people up for disappointment. You chose the latter, so Greg grabbed you and started kissing your neck. He whispered huskily, "Is this disappointing?"

Was that a great night, or did you just imagine it?

"Of course it was a great night!" Greg says now, begging you to understand. You're standing by his kitchen counter, and you grip it to steady yourself. Maybe concentrating on small things can stop the room from spinning. Shiny hardwood floor. Bananas and avocado in a glass bowl. Greg's corn-chip smell. "You're amazing but . . ." he continues, "I just had an epiphany in the desert. . . . Oasis and I have a connection . . ."

You feel like you're in a bad dream. Here's Greg—that big, stubbly, endearing bear, but he looks strange now. You know he always has stupid epiphanies when he takes stupid mushrooms in the stupid desert. You just thought this year his epiphany would be that he wants to marry you because you are the only woman he ever wants to see naked for the rest of his life. The chasm between your fantasy and this actual moment is unbearable.

"What can I say?" you ask bitterly. "How can I argue with a hallucination you, had in a hundred-degree heat on drugs? Obviously this is a great decision for an eighteen-year-old—oh wait! YOU'RE FUCKING THIRTY-FIVE."

Greg shifts uncomfortably. You are doing the worst thing, and you know it. You're being hostile and caustic and highlighting the ugly (albeit limited) ways you are inferior to Oasis. But you can't help it! Doesn't Greg know how much you love him?

"I can totally understand your perspective," Greg says, and his new serenity is taking *annoying* to a new level you never dreamed possible. You hope together they choke and die from high-fructose corn syrup withdrawal. He puts his hand on your shoulder and you shrink back. Sure, you long to snuggle against his big reassuring chest, but then what?

If you can't help yourself and have to touch him again, turn to page 29, section 9.

If you'd rather leave with a smidge of dignity, turn to page 15, section 4.

2

Impish architect Benjamin was a great choice! You love his mischievous smirk—he looks like he's perpetually about to throw a surprise birthday party or rob a bank. Sure, he seems a little emotionally reserved, but what guy isn't at first? The only trouble is . . . he's a dirty talker.

"Oh fuck yeah," he says on your fifth date, for you have decided it's mature to wait until the fifth date to Give It Up.

Benjamin is rolling on the condom while staring at your naked body so intensely that you blush. "God, I want to fuck you so bad," he says. "You hot wet nasty little . . ."

You can't hear the rest because your ears are ringing. You know what's supposed to come next: You're supposed to say stuff back. You're supposed to act porny. But you are not porny; you're just horny. And even *that* word makes you uncomfortable—it reminds you of eighth-grade boys with braces and purple clusters of chin acne who couldn't stop looking at your breasts. So you just say, "yeah yeah yeah" in this really stupid whisper-moan. Then you forget about the dirty talking and just enjoy the ride.

The fact is, you don't think in sentences when you are enjoying carnal pleasures. It may be the *only* time your mind isn't crammed with words and questions but rather just waves of sensation.

When the deed is done, Benjamin spanks your bottom on his way to the shower. You don't know if it's a football spank (*good job, buddy!*), a proprietary lover's spank (*your ass belongs to me now!*), or a punishment spank (*next time, speak up!*). You decide to seek counsel from Crystal, so you meet her at Monsieur Oiseau's for a drink.

"So you're not into it?" she asks.

Crystal is a sexy, voluptuous blonde from a small mining town in Pennsylvania. She can talk as dirty as a beer-swilling, porn-guzzling trucker.

"No, I'm into it," you say, smoothing out the crease in your jeans. "I'm just afraid he's going to expect me to say stuff back."

"Well, yeah!" Crystal laughs and gulps back her drink. "God, I hope this works."

"Are you drinking vodka cranberry juice because of your UTI?" you ask, sipping your too-sweet Appletini. "You should know alcohol neutralizes the effect."

"You're kidding!" Crystal says. "I hate va-drama! So what is he saying? That will help me figure out if you need to say anything back."

"He's just like. . . . Or he's all. . . . Then he like . . ." You can't say it.

"Okay," Crystal understands. She hands you a pen and a wilted napkin. "Write it on this."

You bite your lip and write the first thing Benjamin said as he slid his hand up your dress:

Your ass is amazing.

Crystal laughs, "That's not dirty talk! You could say that!" She's speaking a little louder now, hoping the fedora-wearing guy at the bar will take notice.

"Well, sure," you say. "I'm not a prude. . . . Your ass is amazing." You clear your throat. "Your ass is amazing!"

"Great!" Crystal says.

"Well, it's easier to say to you. Plus, there's more." The next words you write down again.

Suck my rock hard c. I want to f your p. I want to own your p.

Crystal tosses her hair back and laughs. "Fantastic! You said you love it, right?"

"I like hearing it okay, but the idea of *me* saying stuff like that feels ridiculous. First of all, my genitals are clearly mine, not his. At least, legally. And I don't think in sentences like that. It wouldn't be authentic."

"So what?" Crystal asks, signaling to the bartender for another drink. "Fake it till you make it. People take sex too seriously."

You are sure she's right. Crystal is fun and appealing, whereas you feel so grim. It's like *she's* roller skating and *you're* homework. Time to lighten up, lady!

Turn to page 23, section 7.

3

"Shelly," you say finally, because for some reason you are very concerned with being respectful. "Why did you do this?"

"Ya know," Shelly says, fingering a wet curl. "Why not?"

It's a sad thing to say. You and Max walk Shelly back downstairs and insist she take some energy bars for the ride home. "Call if you get lost!" you call after her. "Be safe!"

In bed that night you both wonder about Shelly's home life. Why the hell would she even want to do MCP with two dorks like you guys? The question explodes you into giggles and you snuggle up.

"I love you, dork," Max whispers in your ear. He kisses you deeply, and you throw your arms around him, the way you did the morning of the garbage bags.

So all in all, you could say the event spiced things up a bit and rekindled some passion for you guys. You won't dare admit that Shelly was kind of a drag and not the magical enchantress you had dared to believe in.

In the morning Max gives you a playful little spank. Shelly's butt was toned but your butt is loved, and filled with history. Yours is the butt Max squeezed on your way out of Crate and Barrel. Yours is the butt he squeezed after you went on bike rides to (try to) lose the baby weight. Yours is the chubby beloved butt he wants to squeeze for the rest of his life.

And that suits you just fine.

THE END

4

You take his hand off your shoulder and take a deep breath.

There is nothing left to say, but so much to do. There are so many clothes in his closet, so many shoes, soaps in the bathroom, shampoo in the shower, Q-tips in the drawer, CDs everywhere—the enormity of the task overwhelms you, and you crumple on the kitchen floor in a crying heap. You are still partly outside yourself, aware of how unappealing this picture must be yet unable to do anything else.

"I think you're making a big mistake," you say now, deciding inwardly that you will pick up your stuff some other day, even though you already know you'll need your pajama pants and flip-flops sooner than later. Grabbing them now is just too pathetic. "Actually, I know you're making a big mistake. I'm afraid that by the time you realize that, the window will be closed, but I hope not."

It's a pretty good parting line, one you have been working on all morning, and you hope it seemed dignified instead of desperate.

Turn to page 19, section 6.

Shelly is already flapping around the tub, scales shimmering beneath the silky water. You quickly undress and hop in!

The water could be hotter, but it is okay. Max has always been a sexy guy but seems a bit speechless as he enters the water. For a few minutes you three sit there quietly. Shelly taps her fingers against the side of the tub.

"You really are beautiful," you say, proud of yourself for breaking the silence.

"Then go ahead and kiss me," Shelly says in a *Let's get this going, I have shit to do* way.

You lean in and kiss her softly. A cloud of cigarette smoke fills your mouth. This gets Max excited; he floats over to grab both of your butts. But Shelly doesn't have a butt anymore, or reproductive organs—all such things are buried under the tail. You can't even see the zipper. Shelly's breasts, too, are covered in big plastic shells. So Max squeezes your butt and strokes her tail while you and Shelly kiss, and then you all take turns kissing, and no one mentions that the water has turned a bit tepid. Shelly kisses with a lot of tongue but not a lot of feeling.

There is some fondling and caressing, and it's okay, though embarrassing with forced exclamations like, "Wow, a real

mermaid in our house!" and "This is a miracle!" Also, one wants to take care with the tail—it seems rude to be too rough or presumptuous with it. Finally Shelly tells Max to just go ahead and hump it, and he does, but he slides off in time so as to not disrespect the "magical" appendage.

"Cool," Shelly says and flops out of the water to unzip and dry off. She quickly wraps a towel around her lower body. You and Max turn away to let her change into her clothes. The few minutes feel interminable.

Turn to page 13, section 3.

You hold your head high as you walk out even though your body is trembling and your stomach is churning and your head drops as soon as you're in the car and you're in the fetal position as soon as you reach your bed. For several weeks you can't eat or sleep, which is fine because you remember this from your last broken heart, that awful one, and you know you will live through this, that oxytocin withdrawal will subside if you bear it long enough and hold on, hold on, hold on, reach out to your friends, write about it, drink tea, eat kale, go inward, stay strong, have faith—all those things, all those things—every day for endless days.

Somehow time passes. Summer yields to fall. The sky darkens by six. The fact that you continue to live is a slap in the face to the relationship. Romeo and Juliet never had to find out if they could survive without each other. Just because love means you *want* to die without the other person doesn't mean you *have* to. Your epic tragedy is in fact totally banal. One day you fall asleep on the couch and wake up gasping from an intensely vivid dream: Greg's hand in yours. You feel teary for a moment and then do something strange: You take your own hand. You squeeze it. You press your face against it.

You determine to be your own friend, your own partner. And

this commitment, this realization that *you* will never leave you begins to lift your spirits. You start going out more with your friends, put more energy into work, and even consider going to one of those cardio-barre classes. You don't go, of course, but you think about it.

So now you're ready to get back on OkCupid.

The Internet dating scene hasn't changed much since your pre-Greg years: guys who can't spell, guys who are inappropriately angry, or guys who are forty-five and accomplished, seeking eighteen- to twenty-two-year-olds who enjoy "fun and good times."

You get back into the groove and stomach a string of mediocre dates. Your good friend Crystal advises that you must decode Internet Dating Language. Like if a dude says he wants to "hang out" instead of "take you out," he's just looking for sex. If he says he's

Architect1753

an artist, it means he's unemployed. If he writes too much on his profile, he's overcompensating for something, like that he lives in his car. If he writes too little, he's bland, like he won't like Shakespeare because there's "too much fighting." After a while scanning men's profiles becomes a full-time job.

Part of it is fun, but it can also be baffling and dispiriting. You can go out with a terrific guy and have a truly wonderful night and *then he never calls you again*.

This happens frequently, across all different sites, from Tinder to e-bloody-Harmony. Every eight dates or so you'll have a perfectly lovely time, get really excited, and never hear from the man again. The world of dating is pure anarchy. Plus, your swiping finger is getting sore.

One time you see a cute guy online named Max412 who claims to know the movie *Clueless* by heart like

you do and who even read the Jane Austen book *Emma* that it's based on. You like him, so you decide not to message him back; after all, your instincts have been dead wrong lately. This is the upside-down world you live in now.

"You can't let it break you," your friend Meg says. Her perfect poise and steely determination is why she's a millionaire lawyer and you're a broke French-fry addict. But you like the expression, "Don't let it break you." You repeat it to yourself one night as your eyes grow bleary from staring at the computer.

You're sorting through your new messages (you're now on three dating sites), and you finally notice two guys who aren't bad: *Goodnplenty* and *Architect1753*. The first one has a gentle smile. The second one lists a high income and wears an impish grin.

If heartache has you wanting to be soothed by a gentle smile,
turn to page 171, section 47.

If an employed dude sounds like a refreshing change,
turn to page 9, section 2.

Your seventh date with Benjamin arrives, and you are pumped from the pep talk. You're ready to say some sexy stuff or at least repeat back phrases Benjamin says to you.

He takes you to a high-end sushi restaurant, where you eat spicy salmon kelp rolls and delicate fluke sashimi, perfectly balanced with dried red miso and yuzu sauce. For a moment Benjamin has to text someone for work, so you stuff another piece into your mouth. Then he puts his phone away and looks into your eyes.

"You are absolutely gorgeous," he says.

You smile demurely, cheeks puffy with kelp.

"And that dress is a knockout."

You're glad he noticed the tight aquamarine sheath dress Crystal lent you. It's racier than your usual style, but it seemed like Benjamin wasn't thrilled when you wore jeans and a nubby sweater to the movies last week. You could hold that against him, or you could just enjoy being the Sexy Girl for a change! It doesn't mean you have to dress up like a slutty nurse on Halloween or anything, does it?

"Plus, you're a great writer," he says, as if reading your thoughts. "I loved your piece about how access to frozen yogurt, like access to contraception, is a women's rights issue."

You feel yourself glow. The man is reading your articles. This is definitely *something*. You guzzle some extra sake for courage before heading back to Benjamin's clean, modern apartment. What a lucky girl you are! Benjamin is great—he *deserves* some dirty talk!

Thirty minutes later you're both naked and Benji's getting chatty.

It's P-this and C-that, wet-hot this, and want-to-bend-you-over that. You burn with embarrassed pleasure and get ready for the big moment.

**If you're ready to talk dirty,
turn to page 25, section 8.**

**If you don't want to fake it,
turn to page 159, section 44.**

You take a deep breath and blurt, "I want to feel you inside—my vagina!"

Drat. You pussied out on saying *pussy*.

And "vagina" was a terrible choice—so clinical! *Pussy* is to *fucked* as *vagina* is to *gynecologist*. Why not ask for a pap smear while you're at it?

Benjamin doesn't react poorly. Actually he doesn't respond at all. He just keeps thrusting away. Thank God his eyes are closed so he can't see your face.

Maybe he didn't hear? You want to die or, at the very least, call Crystal. The rest of the sex act goes by in a mortified haze. You squeeze your eyes shut and try to hurry the procedure along so you can both forget it as soon as possible.

Afterward you lay there while Benjamin strokes your arm. You try to enjoy the caress, but you're still blushing from your ridiculous comment. Benjamin grabs his phone and sends another text.

"More work stuff?" you ask. There's silence for a minute or two.

"You know, I'm still pretty serious with my girlfriend," Benjamin says finally.

"Ha ha," you say. You've been busy trying to think of an

interesting new topic to distract from the vagina episode. (Racist police? Fracking? The importance of extra-virgin olive oil?)

"No, I'm serious," he says in his kind tone. "I thought you should know so that, ya know, you could be informed."

You feel dizzy. "Are you serious?"

Nothing is making sense. Benjamin's voice sounds so gentle, but his actual words are awful. Not again. This can't be happening again. You can feel the salmon sloshing around in your stomach.

"Yeah!" Benjamin says, rolling over to his night-stand to pick up his iPad. "It's important to me to be honest." He starts surfing the web.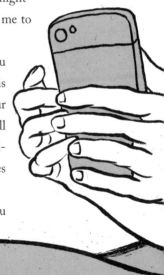

If you were Crystal, you would say, "You want honest?" and smash the iPad over his head. You would say, "Why don't you take your honesty and shove it up your ass?" or "Oh, well it's important for me to tell you and your girl-friend to go fuck yourselves!" These phrases roil inside you, but you can't say them.

Purple with fury and embarrassment, you

scramble to the bathroom to get your clothes and get out of there. Benjamin is a mother f-er, a c-sucking, p-obsessed a-hole. Like so many scoundrels before him, he uses the excuse of "being honest" to honestly be a jerk.

And yet . . . have you brought this on yourself? Did your vaginal faux pas send Benjamin running for the hills?

You'll never know, but it doesn't matter much, does it? After calling Crystal to cry and then watching several hours of *Say Yes to the Dress* on Bravo, you're back where you started: tear stained, alone, and filled with yearning.

"He's out there!" your married friends say gaily. They think dating sounds fun. They are so far away from the loneliness, so far from that thick, hateful expanse of time that stretches before you every night. No one to cuddle. No one to bring you matzoh ball soup when you have the sniffles. How long can you keep your chin up?

If you're ready to give up, turn to page 108, section 31.

If you want to get back out there, turn to page 38, section 13.

"Greg . . ." you whimper and press yourself against him in a hug that feels so good, it hurts.

"It's okay," he caresses your back, and you breathe in his familiar smell with a shudder of relief. You know by his hands that he has finally come to his senses.

"I love you so much," you whisper into his chest.

"Honey, are you in there?" Someone is knocking on the door, someone with a melodic voice and bare shoulders dusted with glitter. Can you guess who?

"Shit," Greg says, but Oasis is already inside because *apparently she has a key*.

"She has a key?" you splutter, immediately withdrawing from the hug. You straighten up and wipe your eyes with the back of your hands. No way this chick is going to see you cry.

Oasis is wearing Daisy Duke jean shorts and a halter top that shows off her tan. She's so tall and skinny that she doesn't need the four-inch platform sandals, but she wears them anyway *because she is the devil*.

"Hiii," she croons. "I've heard so much about you."

"You have?" you mumble pathetically. Her legs are so long, it's tedious.

"Of course! I hope you'll Facebook me." She, the destroyer of your dreams, would like to be besties.

"I'm not much of a social media person," you say. Hours squandered taking quizzes and looking at your friends' drooling baby pictures notwithstanding, that is somewhat true. What's not true is the way you're pretending to be a person when you feel like a corpse. Greg has just lodged a bullet in your heart, and you're talking Facebook with a fetus named Oasis.

Are you that out of touch with reality that you missed the signs with Greg? Are you that desperate that you fell for someone who could love an Oasis? Is Greg insane, or are you? Either way, you're headed for weeks of sobbing in the fetal position. Your little pink heart is dying.

It's time to call a therapist.
Continue to page 31, section 10.

Your new therapist, Dr. Stein, has flowing gray hair and wears no makeup, like a good witch or a ceramics teacher. She congratulates you for being willing to Do the Work as you grieve your broken heart. But let's face it: in the past six months one weekly hour of therapy is all the "work" you've done. You haven't gone out to a new restaurant to review a dish in weeks, choosing instead to churn out angry nonsensical tirades about how finger foods are immature and why almond milk is afraid of commitment. The magazines and websites that normally request your work are growing disinterested.

You're off the dating market and not interested in making plans with your friends, most of whom are married and doing Tubby Time or playing with a Diaper Genie or whatever the hell all those parents do. Meanwhile you've become brilliant at doing nothing.

Today you're on the couch, blasting the air conditioning, gorging yourself on Entenmanns's chocolate-frosted doughnuts. (Hmm, there's an article idea: *Why Entenmann's are still better than Fonuts and Cronuts, you LA douchebags.*) When you get thirsty, you gulp down a glass of cheap red wine. You are reading a trashy magazine, smacking your lips at the article about a starlet's jail sentence. You think it serves the ingénue right: Celebrities shouldn't be allowed to flout society's rules. But you are flouting them too. You're broke, barely employed, and single—and not doing anything about it. The landline rings.

"Hi Mom," you say, breaking off a piece of your third doughnut.

"What, you're still sitting in your apartment?" your mom gasps.

"If you didn't think I was here, why did you call me?"

"Well, I just think you need to get outside, for goodness' sake."

"I work from home, Mom," you put on your patient voice. "I have nowhere to go."

"Well, I'm sure you have some errands to run," Mom sounds pleading. "And you need to start looking for supplemental income!"

"Mother, it's too hot outside, and I apply for jobs online."

"How are you ever going to meet anyone if you don't—"

You slam down the phone.

First of all, you weren't lying—it's scorching outside and humid too, which is terrible for frizzy hair. Second of all, you never know who might show up at the door. The Thai delivery guy, for one thing. Well, maybe not him specifically. But what if something happened to him, and the actual owner of the store had to make the deliveries? And he was handsome and understood that sometimes the heaviness just sets in? What if he smoothes your hair and tells you that everything will be okay?

You plop back down on the couch, refilling your wine glass. *No television during the day* was Mom's cardinal rule. But you are an adult now and can do whatever you want.

You want to watch reruns of the *Tyra Banks Show*. Today it's about morbidly obese teenage girls. Tyra brought doctors on the show to talk about diabetes. Then she shows video clips of the girls huffing on a stair-climber and growing breathless after two minutes. The audience is dismayed, but Tyra seems to be enjoying it. She keeps looking for excuses to refer to her own beauty. "Look, girls, I know the treadmill can be hard, and I was a *supermodel*," she says. Or, "Look, this isn't about weight. It's about self-esteem. I mean, even *I* have felt bad about myself," and then she tosses her hair back. The girls sob about how much they hate themselves.

You aren't morbidly obese, but maybe you're getting a little chunky. You tell yourself that this is a good romantic litmus test: if a guy can't handle a few extra pounds, he has no emotional substance.

If you want to order two noodle dishes from the Thai restaurant, continue to page 34, section 11.

If it's time to get out of the house, turn to page 76, section 23.

You decide in favor of the pad thai with chicken and the pad see-ew with Chinese broccoli, even though they are both noodle dishes. Carbs shmarbs.

The delivery guy is not rich and handsome but rather tired and sweaty. He looks as if he's just crossed a brutal desert. You ask if he wants some water, and he does. He doesn't speak very good English, and a long black hair sprouts from the mole on his chin. Still, he's friendly enough. You offer to share your noodles, so the two of you sit on your couch and watch *Dr. Drew*. All these guys are cheating on their girlfriends with the girlfriends' little sisters.

"What's crazy," you say, "is that these women are willing to take the men back." The delivery guy nods. It seems like he's taking all the chicken for himself and leaving nothing but peanuts and noodles for you. When you realize this, you tell him he has to leave, that you're going to a party tonight. Of course there's no party, but that's not the point.

You go back to reading, now with a little surge of pride.

You're turning a corner, doll. Time to write a new dating profile . . . turn to page 38, section 13.

"I can't lie for you, Zack," you say, and he looks at you with the injured eyes of a shelter dog.

Police Officer Ruiz gives Zack a ticket for drunk driving and a date to appear in court. He warns him about the fine and license suspension that await him. But he says nothing about three strikes or any previous record.

Turns out Zack lied about that.

Turns out Zack lied about other stuff too. The marriages. The children. The house in Marin. (Of course, you're to blame for believing the last one.) Zack is a pathological liar. But he swears that loving you was always the truth.

You can't believe that you've allowed yourself to fall into this life of debauchery. In fact, it never even felt like you. It felt like something took over you, something out of your control.

This is what you tell Dr. Stein at least, who has mercifully decided not to charge you for all your missed appointments. Instead, she tells you you've become a sex addict and advises you to join a twelve-step program.

You're positive she's wrong. Yes, something took over you with Zack, but that was a one-time thing—a Zack thing.

Dr. Stein presses the issue, reminding you that the meetings are free.

You relent and find yourself in a sultry church basement, listening to people talk about the way they use sex like a drug to numb the pain. Some of it sounds like what you just went through. Some of it doesn't. There's a lot of God stuff too. You don't know what to think about that. That calm feeling you get in the Redwood forest—does that count as God?

All you know is you are not calm right now. Something strange is happening; you feel buzzy and your skin prickles with warmth. One by one, you're drinking in the men in the group and how unusually attractive they all are. One has glowing bronze skin and sun-kissed hair. One is Jamaican with pectoral muscles erupting through his tank top. One has an English accent and a knowing smirk that sets your soul aflame.

Maybe you'll stay for the meeting.

THE END

Good for you! The past is the past. You decide to get back out there but be smarter this time. That means writing a new Internet profile. But what should your name be? *Olderbutwiser? Loveisawful? Girlswithbadhairneedlovetoo?* Your (only single) friend Crystal tells you to tone it down a bit. She has a new Internet date practically every night and has agreed to come over and help you.

"All the girls on this website have half-naked selfies," you grumble.

"So you'll be a breath of fresh air," Crystal says. She vetoes ten of your name ideas until finally acquiescing to "churlishbutgirlish."

"If someone doesn't like that name, they can go fuck themselves," you say.

"You gotta get your act together, gorgeous," Crystal says. She's from a mining town in Pennsylvania and isn't scared of anything. You've always admired her courage, and she (impulsive with two broken engagements) admires your restraint.

You bite your nails as she reviews the second draft of your profile.

"I see you put in a review of Indonesian eggplant where your autobiography is supposed to go?" she asks, sipping her wine. "At least this picture in a skirt shows a touch of femininity." Crystal doesn't mind that the wine is warm and the takeout Chinese food is cold. She is a true friend.

"I'm totally feminine," you growl and slurp more pork lo mein. The sauce is too salty and the pork too fatty, but it's getting the job done. "The guys on here are the worst! Every single one of them says they love Hemingway and Bukowski. Every single one of them says they work hard and play hard. How is that possible? They all work just as hard as they play? None of them work at a reasonable level of intensity? None of them play in a casual manner? They're either lying or in a state of perpetual exhaustion!"

Crystal soothes your anxiety by ignoring it.

"Oh, here's a cute one," she says, pointing to a guy named *Max412*.

Max412's profile isn't awful. He seems employed, doesn't confuse *it's* and *its*, and claims to know the movie *Clueless* by heart like you do. Plus he's read the Jane Austen book *Emma* it's based on. You feel your heart jump a tiny bit and decide it must mean Max is bad news. After all, your instincts have been dead wrong lately. Instead, you respond to someone who's reached out to you with the screen name *Hereforyoubaby*. It's an absurd screen name, but you and Crystal agree a little sensitive cheesiness might be good for morale.

Onward, romantic soldier!
Continue to page 40, section 14.

One look at *Hereforyoubaby* has your stomach drop, and not in a good way. The man has one of those hipster curly-q mustaches previously reserved for cinema villains. You find it ridiculous. Same for his giant plastic glasses. No glasses or mustache on his profile pic—why does everyone misrepresent?

He has asked you to meet him at an excellent Vietnamese soup place you're familiar with, and he exhibits noticeably gallant behaviors such as pulling your chair out and calling you "fetching." But when it comes to talking, he barely comes up for air to let you say a word.

He even lectures you about the beauty of Vietnamese pho. You offer that you know all about pho—you are, in fact, a food critic. He seems not to have heard you. You repeat yourself with a joke, "I've pho-gotten more about pho than you'll ever know! Seriously, I'm a food critic."

He looks offended and says, "My aunt was a food critic—a workaholic who ate herself to death. It's more common than you think."

You glower into the steaming pho. It's obvious that *hereforyou* is only *hereforhim*. Luckily, the soup has the perfect amount of cilantro, so you can concentrate on it while he waxes philosophical about home-brew beer and the death of the music industry. Cilantro, cilantro, cilantro. Minty, refreshing, lemony cilantro. *Goodnight, thanks for dinner, great to meet you, no, I don't need to be walked to my car.*

Your next million dates are all different but generally equally depressing. Self-obsessed actor dude. Guy with ten start-up ideas. They all have the same problem as *hereforyoubaby*—they talk too much!

Take Zack, for example. He takes you to a bakery for a late-night snack. It's a fun idea, and Zack is pale and beautiful like an aging vampire. But as soon as you take a bite of your recently dethawed blueberry scone, he says, "You should know I've been married before."

"Oh," you say, noting the orange zest in the scone, a pleasing complement to the blueberry. "You didn't mention that in your profile."

"Don't worry—I don't have alimony payments. My last ex married the perfect man. Very wealthy, pretty much lets her do what she wants. I have kids too."

"Oh . . . cool." *Come on, Zack! Kids too?!* you think. *We need to be able to believe in these profiles.* Sure, *you* described yourself as "slender" when "average" might have been more accurate. But everything else was true!

"Yeah, it's working out pretty well. We can get some cookies if you want."

"I'm good with the scone, thanks. That's the only time you were married, right?"

Zack strums his hand on the table. "Actually, I've been married three times. My first marriage was just obligation. She was pregnant, and my mother said it was my responsibility, basically. Then she cheated on me with a friend of ours who was also married. I was devastated. I would take the train an hour and a half early on Saturday morning to get my kids, spend time with them, and then take the loneliest trip back to Brooklyn, staring at the window into the black emptiness of my reflection. Day after day after day."

"Jesus," you say.

"The second wife I met in a rock-and-roll club in New York. I looked at her doing some hard drugs, and I thought, hey, she's the one."

"Oh," you murmur. Maybe you do need another scone. You feel your loose bra strap falling down your arm, but you're afraid to push it back up, like it will seem like you're not listening to his desperate monologue. Zack is so pretty, with that porcelain skin and red mouth. And he smells good, like spicy lavender.

"What I didn't realize was how much she drank. I was really into partying in those days too, but I could keep it under control. When she drank, though, she'd go postal. If I left the toilet seat up, she'd break a vase. After two and a half years of marriage, it was terrible."

Zack gets up to put milk in his coffee, and you sigh. Zack's profile said he was a music composer who likes quiet evenings and reading the *New York Times*—not making their scandal section. You're about to cut the date short but Zack returns and immediately resumes speaking.

"We went to this Jungian analyst together, and the therapist actually suggested we separate, which was great. I actually toyed with the idea of asking the therapist out, but I didn't. 'Cause I didn't want someone who could analyze my dreams."

Why are you listening to this nonsense? Is it because the green of Zack's eyes is endless? Or because his voice is as gravelly and hypnotic as Idris Elba?

"In the meanwhile I had taken over some of her clients who bought cocaine, and they'd come to our beautiful apartment. Shit got crazy. Five years later I got bottomed out, came back here. Met another woman—Brazilian—incredible. Totally sexual. She came every time she gave me a blowjob and sometimes when she sat down at a restaurant."

You almost choke on your last scone crumb.

"It was just a year, no commitment. We tried again a while later, didn't work. Control was a big thing for her. She was an incest survivor; it was very important for her to feel like she was in control. And there was other stuff that happened, you know, as they do in relationships."

"Yeah—"

"A year later we decided to get married. It felt ideal! I gave my wife money to start a career as an artist—she wanted to do a gallery show about surviving incest and maybe some greeting cards. But nothing was happening." Zack half-laughs and gives you this intense hungry look. You find yourself swimming in the deep green of his eyes.

"One day out of the blue I get the call 'the marriage is over, I'll pick my stuff up.' I was flabbergasted. To this day I haven't figured out totally what happened. Jesus, listen to me ramble. I can't believe I've been talking this long. You're a really good listener, you know that?"

You plunge your fork into his chocolate layer cake. Zack is clearly the mayor of Red Flag Island. He's narcissistic, probably a drug addict, and totally unstable. Nothing good can come of this.

On the other hand, Zack is gorgeous.

Plus, he's acting like he likes *you*. Bad boys never like you. Somehow they're always looking for someone more unhinged, a chick, who smokes cigarettes and wears leather thong underwear. One time you almost told a gorgeous bass player, "I promise you I'm crazy!" But he could just smell that you pay your taxes on time and floss regularly.

And now here's Zack—brooding, sexy, and wrong. You're seized with the urge to pull him into the bathroom and unzip his jeans.

A fantasy is one thing, but you're too old for this! Get back on track, turn to page 105, section 30.

How long have you been cooped up eating Tofutti Cuties by yourself? Live a little! Turn to page 164, section 45.

"*Sas efcharisto*," you say, which means *thank you* in Greek. You think.

And *efcharisto* leads to *ertho* (come over), so you do.

And *ertho* leads to *o thee mou* (oh my god), as Vladimiros buries his gorgeous mouth in your womanhood and leaves you crying out for *perissotera* (more).

You spend hours in his bed, drinking Makedonikos wine and making frenzied love. Vladimiros flips you on your stomach, on all fours, against the wall. Your cheek is smushed, but you don't care. In one afternoon he turns your body into a pleasure playground. Since you can't communicate with language, your body must speak for you. Your body weeps *perissotera, perissotera, perissotera.*

And then his wife walks through the door.

And she doesn't look very happy. Vladimiros immediately straightens up and wraps blankets around his body, leaving you standing there, naked and horrified. His wife starts screaming, and Vladimiros starts screaming too. You don't understand what he's saying, but you get the gist.

Back at the hostel some locals tell you you've been a victim of Greek "kamaki," which refers to a harpoon that catches a fish in one stroke. Then, presumably, doesn't care about the fish anymore. Too bad, because you were very careless about protection, weren't you?

A couple of weeks later, on your last day in Greece, you float in the bright turquoise ocean. The beaches here have the kind of captivating beauty that Vladimiros did—a beauty you can lose yourself in. But you shouldn't really be in the water since you are expecting your period at any minute.

Expecting . . . but not getting.

Not today.

Not tomorrow.

Not in three days when you're flying back to America.

On the taxi drive home you stop at the pharmacy to pick up ten different pregnancy tests. And a candy bar. By the time you burst through your door, you're simultaneously exhausted, jet-lagged, and in a state of total panic. You need to know *right now* if you're pregnant. Or right after you check your Facebook messages.

Friends miss you, friends like your pictures of food, and then there is a very funny message from someone claiming to seek his "lost puppy."

Tire guy!

Apparently he found you through the miracle of social media.

Now all you need is one more miracle—like the courage to

face that pregnancy test. Or the confidence that you can make a beautiful future for yourself, no matter what the results. Or maybe the miracle will be that tire guy is the man of your dreams. And he is just dying to be a father . . .

THE END

16

Getting ready for a date with someone you might like is a terrible thing.

Maybe there were times when you used to enjoy it, but you can't remember them, and you curse yourself for comparing yourself to airbrushed billboard models who look like underfed nympho zombies. Stupid insecurities are such a waste!

But that's not what makes getting ready so terrible. What makes it terrible is that with each stroke of the blush brush, each pluck of an errant brow hair, you are investing more and more into a relationship that hasn't even begun. The act of getting ready for a date is a prayer, like people who dance so that God will make rain. It conjures the hope you've worked so hard to keep dormant in the innermost chamber of your heart. It brings that hope rushing right back up, so if it doesn't go well, the disappointment is crushing. Yes, guys usually pay for first dates, but does that compare to a rain dance?

Tonight, although you're scared to admit it, Max seems cool, at least as much as you can tell over two old fashioneds in a noisy bar. The place is meant to look like a speakeasy, and you give Max two points for a cute pick. Max himself is cute—slender and nimble like Aladdin. He's shorter than you usually like, but there's something confident about him. He seems to be sensitive without sniveling. He's a reader, like you, and was recently laid off from his job as a public defender due to budget cuts. He's still got a positive attitude and doesn't want to quit fighting the good fight. You'd like to know more, but tonight you're focused on yourself.

It scares you—this not knowing what comes next. It's scary that for two years Greg meant everything, and in three years he'll probably mean nothing. What even worse may lie ahead? Will you find great happiness with Max or someone else, or will you be miserable forever and say, "Oh well, at least I wrote a pretty good piece about Balinese duck confit and never murdered anyone."

This is what you're thinking, but thank goodness you don't say any of it to Max. If there's one thing you learned from your mother, it's how to fake being peppy. But the funny thing is, you get the feeling you *could* tell all this stuff to Max. You get the feeling he might understand.

So you're happy when he asks you out again. At the very least, it's a relief to know you haven't totally lost your game.

Unfortunately your second date is a mediocre brunch of bland egg-white omelets and too-sweet mimosas at some overpriced Beverly Hills joint. Afterward Max says, "Do you mind if we stop in Crate and Barrel? I have to pick up a citrus juicer."

You force a smile and say, "Sure," though inwardly you roll

your eyes. Errands? On a second date? You know women are supposed to do hula-hoops for the false intimacy such chores imply, and maybe pre-Greg you would have jumped at the chance, but not anymore. You have your own errands to do—who needs this? And why did Max choose Beverly Hills of all places? Isn't he out of a job? There are more fake breasts and spray tans on this street than a whole season of that new extreme plastic surgery reality show that is beyond offensive. And you should know because you watched the whole season.

Ugh, look at this creature walking in—black leather leggings and ten-inch heels *to go to Crate and Barrel?* And the schlep she's with is dressed like a homeless person! Can someone give you a break? Max glances at the woman, but if he likes babes like this leather-clad lunatic, he is barking up the wrong tree.

Cool it, you tell yourself. *Take it easy!* No wonder some of your friends say you're getting bitter. On the other hand, is there really a healthy midpoint between bitter and naïve? And why the hell does Max need a juicer? Does he not realize there is no fiber in juice?

"My dressings have a lot of citrus in them," he explains, "but I keep getting seeds in there. Like I made a kale salad, and I had all these lemon pits I had to pick out with a spoon. And I've got some even more fascinating stories, if you can believe that." He smiles at you.

You know that Max has only recently taken up cooking, so it's funny how he calls them "my dressings" already. What an ego on this guy!

You sigh and finger some red ladles. They match your sundress with bright cherries on it. You've been wearing optimistic clothing to counteract your recent scowling problem. You hadn't meant to become so sour, but single life is wearing you down. You remember being a very sweet child. And you remember being sweet with Greg—before he exhaled you from his life. If someone throws you out, does that mean you're garbage?

"Are you finding everything you want?" chirps a woman who screams efficiency. Perfect makeup, a clipboard and headset, heels that go clickety-clack. Her eyes are tired, though.

"Actually, I'm looking for a mechanical stainless-steel citrus juicer, but I only see electric ones," Max says.

"Let's just see what we can do about that." The saleslady zips over to the computer and types furiously. "We should have one in stock in the back."

Perhaps sensing your irritation, Max says, "Don't worry about it—I can come back another time."

"No!" the saleslady says. "I'll be right back!" She sprints to the backroom and produces the juicer with astonishing speed. She starts wrapping it with brown tissue paper.

"Oh you don't need to wrap it," Max says, but she counters,

"No, I *do* need to!"

You notice the urgent tone of her voice and move beside Max at the counter. You decide to smile at him, having read that one can activate happy neurons by smiling.

When the saleslady starts printing the receipt, Max says, "Oh, that's really not necessary," but the saleslady says, "No it is. You are not leaving here without everything going perfectly."

She sounds like she's on the verge of tears. Whereas you had been inwardly mocking her a few minutes ago (a headset? seriously?), suddenly you feel a fierce kinship with the woman.

You recognize the sound in her voice, that mixture of desperation and fatigue. You can see the woman fastening her name tag day in and day out, wondering how she ended up selling muffin tins, wondering what her mother would say if she were alive, wondering whether her ex-husband had ever loved her at all, wondering how the same little girl who loved science fairs and crushed it at the eighth-grade debate contest wound up so far away from the sparkly life she had envisioned. You want to hug her and cry with her about everything.

You doubt Max has the empathic accuracy to pick up on this. You read somewhere that many men lack this vital quality. But Max looks the saleslady right in the eye and gives her a warm smile.

"Thank you," he says kindly. "I bet this place would fall apart without you."

The saleslady stands up straighter and her eyes gleam.

"It's my pleasure," she says.

Max turns to you, but you can barely meet his gaze, so humbled are you by his goodness.

The search is over—this guy is the one!
Turn to page 69, section 21.

The timing is just wrong—you're obviously still a train-wreck.
Turn to page 60, section 18.

17

Congratulations—you're smart enough to have figured out that Greg only wants what he can't have. No take-backsies!

Plus, Claude makes you feel so accepted and loved. How have you gone without that for so long?

"He's perfect!" you tell your perfect friend Meg.

She tells you to stop putting people on pedestals.

She's right, of course. Over the next several months Claude reveals some of his flaws. He snores, for one thing. And it would be nice if he could pick up the newspaper once in a while instead of one of his cycling magazines. And he never admits to being afraid.

Unlike some of your past dudes, Claude has no problem expressing love and tenderness toward you (and his daughter, Amy). But he seems to have a problem admitting weakness in himself, even making stupid excuses for his protruding gut, like that the calorie counts on his instant oatmeal packets are lies.

Maybe this posturing is a French thing, but you have to be very careful with someone who has a child. You can't get too involved unless you think you'll be able to be there for Amy for the long haul. She's such a sweet and spunky kid, and tonight when Claude tucks her in, you feel a surge of love for her. The question is, *Do you love Claude?*

You've only been pondering this a few minutes when Claude starts snoring, which doesn't bode well. If you can fall asleep first, the snoring doesn't bother you too much. But try to fall asleep while he's snorting and snorkeling—who could do that? You decide to turn on the small lamp and read for a while, hoping he'll let up. Your book is about a teenage girl who thinks she's a mermaid and is in love with an alcoholic vet. You need to wake up early tomorrow, but you can't stop reading. At twelve-thirty the bed shifts back and forth beneath you, silently.

You leap out of bed and crouch under the desk. Claude undroops one eyelid and laughs. "What are you doing?"

"It's an earthquake!" your heart races and your throat feels dry.

"It's okay. It was a small one. No big deal." Claude has become the king of No Big Deal. Since nothing ever scares him, it makes you seem crazy. Claude checks up on Amy, but she has slept right through it. Fine—maybe you do have a high startle response, but most human beings experience fear. Claude's stalwart attitude is becoming a turn-off.

"It's okay, *belle-fille*. Come snuggle me. *Viens ici*." Every time you mentally prepare to chuck him, Claude turns adorable. Plus, the room has stopped moving.

"Well, I'm going outside just to be safe. You should come with me." You collect some water bottles from the kitchen, pull a sweatshirt over your threadbare nightgown with pig snouts on it, and slip out to the street. Claude calls out, "*Belle-fille*, you don't have to do that!"

The night air is balmy and dipped in moonshine. No one else is out here, which makes you feel stupid. Obviously you are over-reacting. Still, why don't under-reactors get as much criticism? You don't want to return to the little beach house just yet. You'll wait until Claude is snoring again, which will probably be five seconds from now.

Suddenly the ground shakes again, this time with violence. You heave forward, your forehead scraping the asphalt. "Shit," you say, breathing heavily. The ground still shakes and a roaring sound fills your ears. Now people are sprinting outside, scream-ing, carrying puppies and wailing babies. A car has crashed into the pole of a power line. Amy runs to your side and grabs your hand.

"*Ma petite!*" Claude strides out when everyone else runs, his face serene when everyone else's furrows—until a tree collapses on him. You blink, unbelieving. Claude's body is twisted and he grimaces in pain. He is stuck.

"Claude!" you scream and run toward him.

"Get help," he gasps. "My back is fucked. Don't lose Amy."

You scan the chaos for some big guys, but everyone is running around like chickens with their heads cut off. You run back to

Claude, your fear overrun by grim determination. Claude's face is ashen.

"Daddy!" Amy cries.

You lunge your legs forward and push the tree trunk, to no avail. Your face is beet red. You push again. Nothing.

You need help, damn it!
Turn to page 146, section 40.

If you never met a challenge you couldn't overcome,
turn to page 144, section 39.

18

You wish you were stable enough to keep dating Max, but it looks like there's still healing to be done. You need a little more cocooning before you can butterfly. And then one night your life changes forever when you fall into a mud puddle.

You're walking out of your therapist Dr. Stein's office, no less. But any hard-earned morsel of positive feeling you gained in fifty minutes of bellyaching is lost as soon as your ass hits the dirty slop in the middle of the parking lot. It's your own fault for texting (your mother) while walking. Wait—you're supposed to stop blaming yourself for things. But this was clearly your fault—are you supposed to stop blaming yourself for things that are actually your fault?

Dr. Stein would say no, but she would "question the usefulness of blame." And Dr. Stein doesn't think it's your fault that you haven't gotten married yet. She knows it's hard in Los Angeles, a city you hate more with each smoggy breath. You're sick of the traffic, the yoga pants, the trendy restaurants that only serve small plates—can no one eat a T-bone steak and a baked potato anymore? You're sick of coming home to watch TV by yourself while eating peanut butter straight out of the jar.

Today Dr. Stein told a story about how one person went to a

hotel in a new town and found everyone there to be a jerk, and the next patron went to the same hotel in the same town and found everyone there to be a delight. The only difference was . . . their attitude! Can you believe you had to pay money for that?

Anyway, there was no way Dr. Stein was going to win today—you are determined to be in a bad mood. You burned your toast this morning, your mother is texting you incessantly about your biological clock, and now this—stuck in a mud puddle and thoroughly soaked since you spent all this time silently cursing the universe. Such a shame, because you really like the tan linen slacks you are wearing. You trudge to your car and get on the freeway, where you get to drive zero miles an hour in soggy pants. It will probably take you two hours to get home. Then again, what else do you have to look forward to anyway? As your mood grows ever darker, your front left tire grows ever flatter and then just gives up in the middle of the freeway. What a day you are having!

But then something happens just like in the movies. A ruggedly handsome man appears out of nowhere to help you change your tire. He's so large that at first you think you may have encountered your first giant. He doesn't mind that you are bawling. He doesn't mind that you don't have a spare tire. He notices your pretty pants are wet and says you probably deserve a nice dinner. Can you believe he seems kind, thoughtful, and down-to-earth? Well, he might be. And can you believe you two will fall madly in love and you'll be married within the year?

Yes, you believe! Love conquers all! Continue to page 64, section 19.

Not falling for it. Turn to page 198, section 54.

Hooray! You believed in love, and it came true! You are cocoa for cocoa puffs for your tire hero, Jeff. At first it's mostly lust. Jeff is a Marine, which means he's so strong and tall and broad-chested, it triggers a primordial cave-woman lurking within you. Some ferocious inner primate that grunts, "Man kill cave intruders. Me want man."

But as you get to know him, it turns out he is sweet and gentle and even sentimental. He's got a thing for antique quartz miniatures. And he needs his socks color-coordinated in the drawers. And when you're wrapped up in his strong arms or laughing over biscuits with jam in the morning, you feel a peace you have never known.

After eight months, when Jeff falls to his knees at an Ethiopian restaurant you dragged him to—you don't even wait for him to ask the question. You just sit on his knee and bury your head in his neck.

"Yes," you murmur.

Continue to page 65, section 20, cave lady!

Jeff is a simple fellow, which means you have a small, uncomplicated wedding with immediate relatives and a few friends in your mom's garden. Crystal helped you pick out a cream-colored vintage flapper dress. Jeff tells you you're the most beautiful creature in the world, and for a minute you're tempted to believe him.

You move back to Jeff's lovely hometown in North Carolina, which suits you. People are friendly and authentic and consider you very worldly. You make some great friends, who help you create a popular food blog called *In a Pickle* because apparently everyone here loves pickles. You may even have a tip about helping someone open a restaurant! And you have a beautiful baby daughter named Corolla, named after the car that broke down that fateful night. Finally you feel at home and complete.

Well, if this were a movie, it would end right here: *happily ever after*.

In reality, Jeff's Marine unit ends up being moved to Japan, which is hard on the relationship. For one thing, you are only an occasional sushi eater, and that is a serious problem. And you don't speak Japanese, which makes Jeff and Corolla your only friends. You don't have a job anymore. You're thinking about writing some kind of online journal about being an ex-pat, but it's amazing how many others have already done the same thing. You probably have nothing new to add to the genre. Even your seething hatred of Hello Kitty is unoriginal.

Plus, much of what makes Japan exciting—the high-rises, the noise, the nightlife—stresses you out. It's not all tea-sipping and bonsai-snipping, an upsetting fact that reveals you are either racist to have assumed that or have watched the *Karate Kid* too many times (or both). Moving to Japan also breaks your mother's heart, especially when you quickly get pregnant again.

This time you panic right along with your mom. How can you be pregnant on the other side of the world, so far from everything you know? What kind of life will your children have if you never know where you'll be deployed next—Afghanistan or Hawaii? How will you communicate with your doctor for the next ten months? (You learned last time that pregnancy actually lasts ten months—why do people keep saying nine?!)

Your husband tries to soothe your frazzled nerves, but he can never understand how scary it is to be pregnant, let alone in a strange country. Plus, you do not have the hardy disposition of a Marine. Sometimes it feels like he doesn't get that. Which makes you want to smash his favorite quartz elephant, Trunky.

One day, when you are making a little Bento box of snacks for Corolla, you notice tears slipping into the seaweed. *This is only temporary*, you tell yourself.

You Skype your mom, who just cries along with you.

You Skype your dad, who says, *life is a crapshoot—why do you think I'm on my fifth wife?* It's a stupid joke, but you love him for making it so you can laugh for a second. You wish your dad were here now. Even though you rarely even saw him in the States, as he travels constantly, you remember him tucking you into bed at night when you were a kid. You remember his reassuring smell— a combination of cigar smoke and Chiclets chewing gum. By the end of the call you're sobbing in your futon. Everything is new. Everything is weird.

You remember those old relaxation tracks Dr. Stein made for you, the ones that say that no matter what happens, you can handle it. You start listening to them every day. Dr. Stein used to say that resilience is something we cultivate, not something we're born with. And this is an important attitude to have because your second child turns out to be cross-eyed, which is first scary and then stressful. It also brings out a nurturing aspect of Corolla's personality that warms all of your hearts.

In fact, Corolla is such a wonderful big sister that she becomes the spirit guide for the whole family. You learn to lighten up and appreciate the little things, like cherry blossoms blanketing the street during spring. Even on the lousiest days Corolla picks up the baby and says, "Baby! Your face smells like raindrops!" and you all crack up. Or Corolla reads to the baby from *Tales of Frog and Toad* and does funny voices for each character. Or Jeff takes your face in his hands and lets you breathe. You don't know how long you'll be here, but you know now that you can handle it.

And here, once again, a mud puddle was actually a blessing, depending on how you looked at it. And in that sense Dr. Stein's hotel story wasn't so bad after all.

THE END

21

You know a good thing when you see it, so you pull your act together and open up to Max. Sometimes he's corny or obnoxious, but while one part of your brain is criticizing him, the other part of it is learning something very important, something you didn't realize with Greg and previous boyfriends: it's not enough to be dazzled by a man; he has to be dazzled by *you*. And he has to actually *be good at partnership*—listening, expressing feelings, taking you into account before making decisions. These aren't glamorous traits like being impossibly witty or Clooney-like, but they're the stuff that actual working relationships are made of. The more you quiet your little judger, the more Max enchants you. You've figured it out!

You two fall madly in love and start spending every minute together. When you're apart, he sends you emoji of hearts, kissy-faces, and rainbows. You send back hearts, kissy-faces, and baby chickens. Swooping declarations of love are made over crème brûlée. Even going to the movies or grocery store is intoxicating when you're with Max. In the movie theater he licks the butter off your fingers and throws popcorn at you. It feels like the most hilarious and fun game that was ever invented. In the grocery store you kiss in the frozen foods section and wonder if Cathy and Heathcliff from *Wuthering Heights* ever felt such passion. Everything is glorious when you're in love—even taking the garbage out is glorious when you're in love!

In fact, your heart is actually racing one night when you're both carrying smelly garbage bags stuffed with dried egg salad and leftover lemon fettuccini. Something funny is in the air. Max has his head buried in his garbage bag, mumbling about losing something, and then his head pops out, along with his hand, which holds a ring.

He barely gets the words out before you grab the ring and embrace him passionately, no matter that he smells likes garbage. Your moment has finally arrived. You live happily ever after . . . for a good long while.

Continue to page 71, section 22.

22

Disney movies and rom-coms promised you that happiness is a destination you definitively reach when you say *I do* . . . but it's not exactly like that, is it?

The first few years are fantastic. You're thrilled to be in the married club, and there's a lot of morning sex, exciting dinners, and all the cuddling you could ever want. But after a while, well, morning sex is sort of a hassle. Your muscles ache after sleeping, and you really want to get out of bed and do some stretches. You can have sex whenever you want now, which means now is never the perfect time. And eating out is great, but you're usually scribbling on your notepad about the food instead of gazing soulfully into Max's eyes like the old days.

Cuddling is still awesome, and Max squeezes your butt a lot, but it turns out the phrase "the honeymoon is over" is not just a cliché. Banality trumps romance. You used to talk about how good it felt to hold each other or how haunting the moonlight was. Now you talk about the incessant yapping from your neighbor's dog. Or you complain about your broken toe, which you stubbed against Max's dresser. And then Max gets kidney stones and acts like a big baby while you experience the TEN months of vomiting, peeing, and inflammation that is pregnancy.

And once your darling son, Artie, is born—forget it. No matter how much you both try to keep the romance up, life is mostly about the kid. You've given up on cute clothes since they're always spit up on. Some nights you vow to throw on a dress and maybe some heels, but you're just *so tired*. Parents who constantly complain about exhaustion used to drive you crazy, but now you understand. Mommy Tired is a different kind of tired. It's bone-deep.

Still, it's a happy fatigue, and you're okay with the status quo. After all this, this is just what you said you always wanted.

And then one night Max tells you something strange. *There is a mermaid at his gym and she's interested in a threesome.*

You burst into laughter. "Ha ha. You wish."

Max whips out his Google Glasses and shows you a picture of a beautiful young woman alone in a steam room. Jet-black curls cover her breasts, but beneath her belly button is an unmistakable purple tail. It's crazy, it's absolutely ridiculous, but it's right there. Apparently Max had accidentally walked into the women's room and spied the lovely creature. They got to talking, and soon an offer was on the table.

Your feelings are mixed. You believe in marital fidelity, but this *is* an unusual circumstance. And though you aren't terribly lesbian, does a mermaid's gender even count? Even if you weren't into it, wouldn't Max resent you for the rest of your life if you don't give it a shot? At least he's including you. Plus, you have to admit the image of a magical creature disrupting your banal world of diapers and deadlines is a little . . . titillating.

So you set the date for a week hence, and excitement starts buzzing inside you.

"I have to admit it's flattering that a mermaid would be interested in us," Max says on The Night, squeezing your butt.

"I know!" you respond in good fun. Your stomach is full of jumping beans.

Not long after your mom picks up Artie for Grandma night, Shelly the mermaid arrives at your door. Dry, she looks like a pretty and sullen college kid with a pouty mouth and lots of black eyeliner. She wears jeans and a black tank top, and her cell phone rests comfortably on her hip. Her curls are clipped into a messy bun.

"So you wanna get started?" she asks. She tugs at the gym bag hanging on her shoulder.

You and Max are both surprised at her demeanor. It's not like Shelly is a prostitute—was this some kind of dare? Is she mocking you? You've been imagining fascinating wine-soaked conversation about Shelly's unusual life. But Shelly denies the aged Gruyere and Petite Sirah (apparently both lactose intolerant and a sober alcoholic), and the three of you awkwardly make your way to the upstairs bathroom.

While the tub fills with steamy water, Shelly sits on the edge and smokes a cigarette.

"Oh, I'm sorry, you can't smoke in—" you begin, but Max cuts you off, saying surely you can make an exception. You nod nervously and gulp more wine.

When Shelly finishes her cigarette, she reaches into her gym bag and pulls out a giant purple tail. She unzips her jeans and tugs them off. You are crestfallen.

"So you're not really a mermaid," you say, idiotically.

"Of course I am," Shelly says.

"That's a costume," you point out as Shelly swings her legs into it.

Shelly leans forward in an irritated whisper. "What are you doing? I thought you guys were into MCP."

"Sssh, honey," Max says.

"MCP," Shelly continues. "Mythical Creature Play. I thought that's what this is about. You're supposed to go along with it."

You feel blood pounding in your temples. Mommy Tired equals Mommy Stupid. How could you not have realized? But if Shelly isn't a mermaid, this is just Greg and Oasis all over again. It's just another man wanting to have kinky sex with a pretty young girl. No! Shelly isn't a mermaid—it doesn't count!

On the other hand, kicking Shelly out now means openly admitting you believed this girl was going to turn into a fish.

It's humiliating!

Humiliation Shmumiliation—no freebies for Max. Kick her out, turn to page 98, section 28.

Ah, what the hell? Jump on the MCP train! Turn to page 16, section 5.

23

There are obvious things you should do now, such as exercise, look for a job, or write a Facebook post about how blessed and grateful you are to be going through a difficult time *because this is when you learn the most.*

Instead, you go see an old friend at a comedy show—Lord knows she's posted enough about it on social media. It's nice to hide in the darkness of the crowded theater that reeks of stale beer and cleaning fluid smeared on the tables. Plus, it's only five dollars. Your friend's jokes are mostly about dieting, sex, and her mother-in-law. It's hard to muster up chuckles. But the laughter of the rest of the crowd eases your loneliness. You are all here in search of a smile. You are all here to share in the (almost) universal experience of feeling like a complete loser. You start attending stand-up comedy regularly. You don't laugh much, but you do appreciate the humiliation involved. There's a kinship there.

However, you notice with concern that a lot of comics use the word *vagina* lately. In fact, the word is bandied about everywhere: movies, sitcoms, YouTube videos. Your problem with the vagina thing is that no one is using the word correctly. The female genitals are not vaginas. The hole is the vagina. The whole thing, the external genitals, that's a vulva.

You want everyone to say vulva, you want your mother to stop asking if you have met a man yet, and you want it to be okay that you won't wake up early enough to spruce up your limp hair. Is this too much to ask?

Let's face it: You are not drop-dead gorgeous. You're just kinda cute and adequately proportioned. That's not easy in Los Angeles. Is it anywhere?

Your mom says it's fine, *just remember you never know who you're going to bump into at the supermarket*. But you *do* know who you're going to bump into at the supermarket—Luis, the guy at the register. He's married, like everyone else. You would like to be married too, but you don't want to doll up every time you buy frozen chicken nuggets. You like to be relaxed and authentic. Maybe authenticity isn't obviously sexy and that's why Greg preferred Oasis, but you bet a lot of other guys will find it refreshing.

"They might not find it as refreshing as you think," your friend Meg tells you one Sunday night. You are at Meg's opulent Brentwood home, sipping chilled white wine in the master bedroom. Meg is a few years older but light years ahead of you. She's rich, successful, married to a devoted stock analyst, and mother to an adorable dumpling of a child. You'd hate her guts if she weren't one of your best friends.

"The thing you have to realize is that dating in your thirties is a lot different from your twenties."

"Oh that's a revelation," you snap at her. "I know about my stupid biological clock, okay?!" *Who even wants kids anyway*, you say silently. All your friends with kids are perpetually exhausted, cranky, and overwhelmed by drudgery. Then they post baby pics on Instagram about how miraculous it all is. Ugh.

Meg says, "Ssshh, you'll wake the baby! This isn't about biological clocks. But you can't get away with the stuff you did in your youth anymore. You have to start knowing a little about fashion and style."

This you do not want to hear because you've never been great about fashion and style. You never understand when something is blousy or just frumpy and when it is tight/sexy or tight/too small. But suddenly Meg is doing a whole fashion lesson, describing which kind of sneakers are "unacceptable," jeans with "good fades," and "belts." You try to explain that you never wear belts—you fundamentally don't understand them. Are you supposed to purposely buy clothes that are too big so that you can wear a belt? What outfits warrant a chunky versus a thin belt?

"I don't understand the fashion rules," you explain, "especially the one that says there are no rules, because really what that means is that there *are* rules, they're just too confusing to be explained clearly. I can't be bothered with all that. I don't have the time. I've become an avid supporter of the Los Angeles comedy scene."

"Just try this on," Meg throws a bright yellow dress at you. It has loops and compartments and seems like it's from the future.

"I don't even understand where these flaps go," you say, but Meg has stopped listening. She is staring at your body as you pull the dress over your head. Her glossy mouth hangs open in horror.

"What?" you ask.

Meg's jaw clenches grimly.

"Just say it!"

"Okay," Meg breathes slowly, trying to calm herself down. "What is that underwear?"

You look down and chuckle fondly at your ten-year-old Costco panties. "What? Are they really bad or something?"

But Meg is truly horrified. "*They're homeless-people underwear.*"

You laugh again. You know you should feel the standard female levels of shame and self-hatred, but you really don't understand what your friend is saying.

"What's so bad about them?"

"There are holes in them! They're falling apart!"

You look again as though in a fog. There *are* holes, they *are* falling apart, but you're having a hard time grasping what's so bad about that.

"I mean they're not unflattering," you say. "My body looks okay—you know, for a normal woman. They're not lingerie or something."

Meg is just as confused as you.

"I don't understand what's going on here," Meg says. "You need to throw those out. Does all your underwear look like that?"

"Well, some are worse," you say. "These aren't period underwear."

"You have more than one pair of underwear with holes in them?" Meg starts ransacking her meticulous underwear drawers, grabbing pretty, lacy panties and throwing them at your face.

"So it's the holes that are bad?" Your brain feels gooey.

"It's everything! They're like a hundred years old!"

"Oh . . . but, I mean, they still work."

"No, they don't!" Meg struggles to break down a seemingly simple concept. "They're not holding you up. And they bunch up and creep out of your jeans!"

"Well, I pull them down," you say. "Are you saying you just throw out perfectly good underwear?"

"They're not perfectly good!" Meg finally explodes. "They're terrible, terrible underwear! Shit, I'm going to wake the baby."

The two of you stand there.

Your friend: beautiful, fashionable, successful.

You: disheveled, half-naked, wondering if you have enough frozen chicken nuggets left for dinner.

Meg quiets down and takes one last look at your withering cotton friend. "Just get rid of them."

"Okay. I had no idea. I mean, I know they're not like underwear people wear in the movies, but I'm not one of *those girls*."

Meg's frustration has turned to concern, so she gathers some patience.

"You don't have to be one of those girls, sweetie. But underwear is more than a strip of cloth to protect your genitals."

"Ohh," you murmur. "It's weird because that's *exactly* how I think of them."

"No," she urges. "Underwear can actually work for you. It can make you look good in your clothes or be attractive when you're out of your clothes. I mean you're single now . . ."

All of a sudden, finally, it hits you. *You wore this underwear with your ex-boyfriend Greg. This is why he left you for Oasis. Of course—it wasn't his fear of commitment! Does any man even have a fear of commitment, or is that just something women fabricate to feel slightly less horrible?*

"Oh my god," you say, sitting quietly on the bed. "How could I have thought he didn't care about panties or insouciance? Deep down all guys want one of those girls. I'm not refreshing . . . I'm disgusting." The tears start falling.

"No," Meg says.

"Yes," you cry. "I'm like some weird freak. I've somehow missed the memo on how to live life as a human." You can feel your scalp tingling into the shape of a conehead.

It had never occurred to you that somewhere between being a Victoria's Secret model and a hideous lunatic is some sort of moderate approach to underwear. You just didn't see it.

You know what to do! Get your ass in shape, get some sexy underwear, and get your true love Greg back once and for all!

Turn to page 138, section 38.

So maybe you're a little gross—someone has to find that charming.

Stay true to yourself and turn to page 85, section 25.

24

For some strange reason you don't actually want to savage this Adonis. Yes, there is a passion inside you, but if you listen closely, what it's really asking you to do is . . . *paint a picture of the moussaka at your table*.

What?

You take another sip of ouzo and quiet yourself. You focus again on that stirring in your heart.

Paint the moussaka!

Huh?

Paint it!

It's a strange compulsion, but following your instincts has led to good things lately. A two-day search leads you to a hidden crafts store to buy paints and an easel. You lug them to the balcony of your little hostel and let the wind cool your flushed cheeks. You begin painting, the strokes coming naturally, as if from another person. A divine energy is working through you, bringing the lasagna-like dish from your mind onto the paper in lush, vivid strokes!

From here you enter a state of clear, contented knowing.

You are meant to live in Greece. You are meant to paint food. You are meant to be untethered by romantic entanglements and live as free as the wind. It flutters through your hair now, in tandem with your wild heart.

THE END

25

"Honey," Meg sighs. "People don't break up because of underwear. And if it meant that much to him, he should have said something."

At that moment the baby starts crying, and you are left with your own fevered brain. Your first thought is to call Greg—heart slayer!—to beg him to forgive you and give you a chance to make it right. You can get fun little polka-dotted panties or maybe those shiny, porny kinds . . . but then you think:

If I start wearing perfectly intact underwear, what's next? Wearing skinny jeans to Trader Joe's? Doing a juice cleanse? Getting Brazilian waxes and referring to them as "just keeping tidy"? Where does it end?

Meg's baby crawls groggily into the room, excited that his "auntie" is here. You scoop him against your chest and feel his sweet powdery breath on your cheek. *Maybe being a godmother is enough.* You think of your own three great aunts, how none of them ever married, and you wonder what kind of panties they wore. You decide right now that you can at least commit to throwing away mostly disintegrated clothing—that seems reasonable.

It doesn't much matter because your next boyfriend, J. P., is a terrific guy who says he doesn't care about undergarments at all. And he says that belts are for suckers and that your opposition to whimsy is charming. But then, for your birthday—sexy underwear.

Guys may not be as complicated as you thought.

You tell J. P. that lingerie is a gift for him, not you, and you would have preferred a beautiful teacup. You almost add: *Plus, they aren't even cotton-crotch! You might as well have given me a yeast infection wrapped in tissue paper!*

What stops you is the thought that maybe, on some level, lingerie is a decent gift. Maybe every woman—whether she is beautiful or plain, married or single, quirky and perky, or grumpy and dumpy—maybe you all deserve a beautiful pair of underwear.

"I guess I'll put them on later," you say.

"That's entirely up to you," J. P. says. "I just want your vulva to be happy."

He could be the one.

Have you finally met your match?
Turn to page 87, section 26.

26

You have hit the jackpot, Miss Thang! J. P. is a real adult—stable, mature, and self-assured. He's sandy haired and trim, with a reassuring smile like he could run a Wall Street meeting or clean up a kid's puke, and it will all turn out just fine. You've now been dating for twelve weeks, and they've whizzed by in a colorful blur of avant-garde art exhibits and world music concerts.

Tonight you're munching (rubbery) chicken tikka masala and basmati rice at a new Indian restaurant near his Hancock Park condo.

"This food probably doesn't live up to your standards," J. P. says sheepishly. "I remember it being better."

"Oh posh!" you say, though he's right. The masala sauce is all butter without the delicate interplay of paprika, cumin, and cinnamon that ought to be there. But you don't want to make J. P. feel bad. After all, it's hard to be a man these days. You and your friends still want guys to be powerful and dominant but only in an evolved diaper-changing way. It's a tightrope.

J. P. has walked it well—allowing himself to get teary at a foreign film but assertive in the boudoir. Making you scrambled eggs for breakfast but killing bugs with swift efficiency. There is a lot of late-night soulful talking too. Masala shmasala!

And now he says, "So what do you think about meeting my parents in a week or so? They've done some remodeling and want to show it off."

Your heart scampers inside its little cage. Meet his creators!

"You don't think it's too soon for that?" you ask casually. You don't want to appear too eager about the offer, don't want to be one of those girls who does hula hoops every time a guy steps the relationship forward. At the same time, you want to be sweet and encouraging. It's a tightrope.

"Well, I won't propose that night, how's that?" J. P. winks. Few men can get away with winking, but J. P. is a natural. He's got a law degree from Berkeley and now helps run a company teaching students how to prepare for the LSAT. You wonder how many winks he has to throw at the hordes of anxious students before they can relax and focus on their logic puzzles. Sometimes he sends you a puzzle, but you'd rather curl up on the couch with a Brontë novel.

"Oh, my parents are going to love your whole literature thing. My dad is very into Joan Didion."

"Hmm," you say mysteriously. After a decade of dating, you've decided a little game playing is okay in the first months. Your new goal is to reel them in with your quiet wit and then slowly let the crazy out. It's not like you're truly unstable or anything, but having been tackled so many times on the football field of love, you're a little bruised.

Tonight all the others recede into the background of your mind, with only J. P. shining brightly in the fore. You are two mature adults ready for commitment. You can do this. In the days leading up to meeting his parents you both fall in love a bit more.

The morning of the dinner is uncommonly drizzly. You and J. P. cuddle up on the couch with coffee and the *New York Times* and rain pouring against the window. He breathes into your neck and caresses your soft belly. You feel yourself slipping into that dream state, as though you have been holding onto a bright balloon in the clouds and now are floating away.

You're still wrapped in that gauzy bliss when you knock on the Morettis' door.

"Oh my God, she's beautiful," Mrs. Moretti immediately pulls you into an intense hug. She is a tiny woman, and you can feel her bones press against you. Her face is delicate, and her slacks and silky blouse look like they cost more than your rent.

J. P. winks and takes your hand as you enter an elegant Beachwood mansion.

"What a lovely place," you murmur.

"We should really get a smaller one," Mrs. Moretti says. "WHO NEEDS IT?!" The roar is surprising bursting out of such a small body. What she lacks in flesh she makes up for with sheer lung power.

You smile shyly, and Mrs. Moretti shoves a glass of wine in your hand. "It's from Napa Valley! SIT DOWN!" You note her habit of working toward a yell at the end of any given thought.

You and J. P. sit down next to each other as Mother barks, "BOYS!" and her husband and another handsome man amble in.

"Steve . . . what are you doing here?" J. P. was not expecting to see his lanky, unshaven brother.

"Laid off again, dude. Kathy split. I'm just regrouping."

J. P. has only briefly mentioned his brother to you, something about a distant relationship and a gambling problem. J. P.'s pursed lips do not suggest pleasure at the reunion.

"Regrouping," Mr. Moretti grunts in a thick Italian accent. He is thick, swarthy, and as authoritative as his wife. He settles into his chair. "Mooching is what we call it."

"Fuck off, Dad," Steve says.

"Go fuck yourself," Mr. Moretti says back. They aren't yelling, but they aren't smiling either, and you have no idea whether they are kidding or not. People in your family don't talk this way.

"YOU LIKE SALAD!" Mrs. Moretti barks. It's not a question, so you just take the bowl of dandelion salad placed in front of you. You are mentally rehearsing answers to all the expected questions (What do you do? Do you want kids? Where are your parents from?), but no one asks you anything.

"You know, Dad," J. P. beams at you, "she loves literature. She

used to teach at a high school." J. P. loves hearing stories about your early work as an emergency substitute English teacher. He loves hearing everything about you.

Mr. Moretti's eye twitches. "I know your generation has to be politically correct with all the female authors, but you can't leave out the greats." He pours more wine in your glass.

"Oh, I didn't, sir," you say obediently. "We did Fitzgerald, Faulkner . . . but, yes, we did include important women authors like Flannery O'Connor, Eudora Welty, Toni Morrison . . ." J. P.'s parents exchange a knowing snort.

"Toni Morrison—ugh!" Mother pushes the air with her hands.

"You don't like Toni Morrison?" You hadn't realized this was a debatable issue.

"Garbage!" Mr. Moretti says.

You don't know if it is possible to dislike Toni Morrison without being racist, but at the moment you're scrambling to determine if you should just shrug sweetly or showcase the "spunk" J. P. said they would enjoy.

**Keep drinking and stay quiet.
Continue to page 93, section 27.**

27

You guzzle your wine and smile.

"Ever fuck any of your students?" Steve asks, laughing. J. P. shares his mother's fair skin and fine hair, whereas Steve has his dad's olive complexion and thick black hair. There's some resemblance in the brothers' faces, but Steve's is more brooding. You blush.

"Shut up," J. P. warns.

"It's a legitimate question! I mean, they're almost of age."

"Don't listen to him," Mrs. Moretti says. "THERE'S NOTHING WRONG WITH IT!"

"Well . . . even if that were the case . . ." you falter. "I'd never have . . ."

"I'm sure young boys tried to seduce you," Mr. Moretti says, his eye twitching. "No one ever wants to talk honestly about how seductive students can be. Look at all the little temptresses ruining our country."

"Well . . . I'm not sure that's true . . ." You're getting a little light-headed.

"Don't worry, sweetie," Mother says. "We're just busting your balls!" The family all laughs, so you join in. Frankly, you don't know what the hell is going on.

Mother whisks away your salad bowls and replaces them with larger plates teeming with broiled beef ribs smothered in barbeque sauce.

"Jeez, Mom, I told you I'm trying to take it easy on that stuff," J. P. says.

"IT'S LIGHT!" Mother says.

"You like the art in here?" Steve asks, winking at you.

It's only at this moment that you get a closer look at the giant paintings on the wall in front of you. You had noticed their bright red splashes and even the somber look in the faces of the men painted. You hadn't noticed that they are naked and holding their erect penises.

"Wow," you say. "Those certainly . . . make a statement."

Mr. Moretti refills your wine glass again. "They were painted by a dear friend of ours. Some of it may seem over-the-top, but his brushwork is really quite accomplished. That's his stuff behind you as well." You scan a large black-and-white drawing of a party filled with beautiful naked guests having an orgy that includes wolves and pigs. The guests are male, female, and some have both sets of genitals.

"I'm sure that's amazing . . . I don't know that much about art." Nor do you know how to eat ribs without floss, a mirror, and a bib.

"She's churning out food reviews on weekends when she

should be going to museums," J. P. says fondly.

"Why should she go to a museum? Your generation has no WORK ETHIC!" Mother pushes the air again, "your generation" now bumping into "Toni Morrison."

"Is that a jab at me?" Steve asks.

"You're not her generation," J. P. says.

"These ribs are terrific," you say.

"Well done, Mom," J. P. agrees.

"So many barbeque sauces are just political bullshit!" Mr. Moretti says pleasantly. You're beginning to think J. P. is the only sane one in his bunch, but his membership to the herd is disconcerting. Why has he not talked about them more? Why has he not mentioned their eccentricities? What do you really know about J. P. anyway?

Mr. Moretti continues: "So Uncle William's PSA tests came back in. The cancer is gone for now." The family raises their glasses in unison to toast the good news. You wonder if there is something genetic to worry about.

"Now all I need is my cash flow straightened out," says Steve, running his fingers through his thick hair, "and the whole family is back on track."

"Unbelievable—he can even make our uncle's cancer about him," J. P. mutters.

"What? I'm thrilled for Uncle William. I forgot that the great legal scholar never thinks of himself—he's too busy saving the lives of overprivileged law-school wannabes."

"Brothers shouldn't fight," Mr. Moretti says. "It leads to indigestion. William and I never fight, even though he is a complete idiot. I mean, he's fucking useless, that guy."

"Well, he loves the cat," Mother says.

You choose this moment to excuse yourself and stumble drunkenly to the bathroom. You tug your short black dress down so as not to be too exposed. You stare at the painting of a woman framed above the towel rack. The subject is topless with nipples so big and bright red, you feel visually assaulted. The background paper is marbled with a light psychedelic paisley. J. P. once joked that the whole family dropped acid together on New Year's Eve. The realization that he might have been serious suddenly twists your stomach.

You remind yourself that your own family is a few cupcakes shy of a picnic. But will you ever fit into the Moretti clan? What will happen on Christmas—you'll all take mushrooms together and look at pornographic pictures of Santa? *Don't get ahead of yourself*, you tell your reflection. *Just get through the night. Stop judging so much!* Your eye makeup is still holding up well, but you unzip your purse to reapply your lipstick. The action steadies you. *J. P. is a wonderful guy, and this is a great relationship. Lighten up!*

You stride with more confidence out of the bathroom and

march straight into Steve's chest. It is broad and stretches his thin green T-shirt. He smells like wine and grime mixed together.

"Watch where you're going, babe," Steve says roughly. "I wouldn't want J. P. to see you pressing up against me."

"Ha ha—I'm staying out of it," you say, not quite meeting his gaze. But Steve steps in your direction again so you can't get past him without looking right into his dark, gleaming eyes. He pushes you against the wall and kisses you searchingly. You gasp in his mouth but don't push him off. You let the kiss unfold, let Steve slide his hand up your dress and squeeze your ass. Then he breaks off from you and casually strolls into the bathroom.

What have you done, you brazen monster?
Confess your sins to J. P. and beg forgiveness!
Turn to page 103, section 29.

You are an idiot but not stupid enough to say anything.
Keep your mouth shut and get back to your man!
Turn to page 120, section 34.

28

Kicking Shelly out is awkward but necessary. You claim to have suddenly developed a migraine headache and need to lie down immediately. Shelly doesn't seem perturbed by the change in plans—now she'll be able to make it to an AA meeting. Max actually seems relieved and believes you about the headache. Later, when he comes to bed, you pretend you're already asleep.

And life returns to normal. You're working from home and taking care of your son. Max is working long hours at the courthouse now, so you're both still exhausted all the time. But it's perfectly pleasant between you, and if there are invisible resentments hanging in the air, they don't seem worth mentioning.

A few months later there is dried puke on your nightgown when you discover your husband is cheating.

Max has a file on his computer titled L. You're not supposed to go on his computer, and he doesn't even know you know the password—"workingovertime." It's a terrible password. But you are snooping, and that's how you find L.

L is a series of digital photos of a glowing young woman in various states of undress. In a see-through nightie. In black lace bra and panties with a garter belt. Totally naked. Totally naked and touching herself.

L looks twenty years old. You are now in your late thirties. L is tan with perfect skin. You are pale with stretch marks. L looks insouciant. You feel pretty souciant. Is it just that simple?

The room won't stop spinning. Your muscles feel like sandbags. You are weighted down to the chair. There's adrenaline going, but you're also exhausted. You guys have a three-year-old. This is not okay. That's what you tell your son, Artie, sometimes too: *This is not okay*.

"Mommy!" Artie cries. Artie has a poopie in his diaper. Artie makes a lot of poopies. "Yay!" you and Max say because you're supposed to encourage it. Max calls them Superman poopies. Or the person you thought was Max said that. The person you thought was Max now seems blurry. You have no idea what anything is. You could let your son marinate in his own shit for hours while you try to reassemble your brain, but you aren't that person. You tend to your son.

You change his diaper and pour on the baby powder when he begs for more "fairy dust." You make him honey wheat toast with sweet potatoes and spinach. You snuggle him and watch *Clifford the Big Red Dog*. You bury your face into his soft, powdered neck. You hug his little body, and he puts his tiny hand on your knee. It's enough to make you sob, but you choke it back. Meanwhile, Clifford's loyalty to Emily Elizabeth knows no bounds. He'd do anything for her, even dip himself in paint. That dog is fucking amazing. You wish you could jump on Clifford's big red back and ride off into the sunset with him.

Instead, you put on jeans and a crummy T-shirt and take Artie to the park. The kids say, *Gimme! I want it! I don't want to be a good boy!* Everything has a double meaning now. Your stomach churns. You should probably eat something today, but you can't.

The other moms don't seem as exhausted. They're younger. They have personal trainers. Or they're nannies. Some nannies are pretty hot these days. Is L a nanny? A stripper? A bad tipper?

In earlier times there would be no digital pictures. Even simple e-mails would have been better. You can never unsee those photos. A ruddy-cheeked mom agrees to watch Artie so you can run to the bathroom and throw up. Then you rinse your mouth and come right back out to watch your son.

Maybe e-mails would have been worse. E-mails could say, "I can't stop thinking about you." E-mails could say, "I can barely look at my wife—she's so disgusting and tired all the time. If only we didn't have that idiot kid, I'd leave her in a heartbeat." E-mails could say, "I love you."

On the other hand, now Max is in control of the narrative. He can say, "Those are an office joke!" He can say, "I felt bad for her—her mother has a wooden leg." He can say, "It was a terrible mistake—I'll never see her again," but that can be a lie.

Mommy, push me, so you push Artie on the swing. *Higher than an airplane! Higher than a tree! Higher than a giant fish! Higher than a giant meatball!*

During naptime you take a shower but don't wash anything. You just stand under the hot water and wish today wasn't happening. You wish it were yesterday or six months ago. Max had started coming home late, but Max came home late sometimes. You weren't having a lot of sex, but that happens too. You felt off, but you can feel off. There was nothing to put your finger on. And you would never suspect Max of doing something like this. It was completely surreal; he was such a stand-up guy. Whatever his faults—controlling, whiny, grumpy—he wasn't *this*.

In fact, you had been snooping to see if anything was going on with Max financially. Max was the type to hide any concerns in this department. *This* wouldn't have occurred to you. Your mom always said you are too trusting. You try to take in the information, but your mind keeps rejecting it, like a body that rejects an organ transplant. The information does not belong in your cells. It is wrong. It is so wrong, it maybe isn't true? But it is true. It is L. He wouldn't title the folder L if it weren't true.

You stand naked in front of your closet after the shower. What should you wear? What do you wear the day you discover your wonderful stand-up guy is an alien? Is a destroyer of trust? Do you wear something pretty to make him regret it? But this isn't eighth grade—this is marriage. There is a mortgage, there is a child, there is supposed to be an understanding here. So you just put on your green terrycloth robe because there will probably be more puking today, from Artie and from yourself. You put your dirty wet hair up in bobby pins. You make yourself tea and plain toast but can only take two bites. You feel a million years old.

After naptime Artie plays with his toys as you watch from the couch. You feel like mostly a zombie, but you smile when he looks over at you. Artie is being very good, not throwing anything like usual, only making a medium-sized mess. He seems pleased you're not working like you usually are during this period. Or maybe he senses your sadness and is trying to be extra cute. And what are you going to do—run away with your son and raise him by yourself with no money and no father? Move back in with your Vicodin-zonked mother? You're trapped, aren't you? Whatever Max says, it will be words from the mouth of the New Max, so you won't understand them. It's like someone put a giant ox on the table and asked you to eat it. You don't know where to begin.

You got over Greg, you threw out a mermaid—you will get through this too. If you want to leave Max a note and begin a new life, turn to page 196, section 53.

If you'd like to hear what Max has to say for himself, turn to page 149, section 41.

29

You stumble back into the dining room, tears streaming down your face and nose.

"Honey, what's wrong?" J. P. rushes over to you.

"I kissed your brother!" you blurt. "He cornered me against a wall and I just—I don't know what I was doing. It's like I was purposely trying to ruin things, like I'm just so scared to try again, and you're so great, and I just really love you—I think I love you!"

While you're babbling J. P. has turned as white as the wolf in the orgy painting. His parents' mouths hang open, aghast. Steve is smirking.

"I love you too," J. P. whispers, and sweet relief restores breath to your lungs.

"Thank god," you murmur gratefully. "I'm so—"

"In fact, I was sure you were the girl I was going to marry," J. P. continues. "But this is the one thing I can't forgive. Not my brother. I'm sorry."

Mrs. Moretti shakes her head in disapproval with this knowing look like she knew all along you were no good.

"Ah, who cares, bro? Don't throw her away over my stupid ass," Steve offers.

You look at J. P., praying his brother's words will make a

difference. You can see by his stony face that they don't.

"I'm so sorry," you gurgle, but tears are making it hard to talk. "At least I told—"

J. P. is not listening. There is nothing to give except up.

You Uber a ride home, and as you sit in the backseat, your whole romantic life flashes before you in grand majestic sweeps of dog shit. So many mistakes made. So many red flags that should have been noticed or opportunities that should have been seized. You're always doing the wrong thing, aren't you? Isn't that why you're alone? You tip the driver and trudge to your door to find . . .

Turn to page 109, section 32.

30

A few years ago you might have even eaten up Zack's story, hoping to be his Florence Nightingale. But by now you've learned something: it's not his troubled history; it's the fact that he's putting it out there so soon. This is what separates the winners and losers in the dating world—who can keep their crazy quiet the longest.

Zack vaguely notices how much of his cake you've eaten and takes a bite himself. He continues with his mouth full.

"I just didn't know what I needed at the time. I didn't recognize I needed emotional comfort. Even though my last wife left me, she also helped me realize how self-pitying I was, how self-indulgent. My father committed suicide. But my therapist explained that suicide was the peak of a narcissistic personality. I heard that, and it hit me very bad. I thought my problems were about everything around me, but I realize they weren't . . . you know?"

You have an urge to be honest. You'd like to say, "No, I don't know, Zack. This is a crazy story, and you shouldn't tell it to someone on the first date. And you shouldn't lie on your profile. And yes, I've enjoyed this scone and cake, and yes, part of me wants to give you a blowie in the bathroom, but you should ask a woman something about herself sometime."

You're neither mature nor brave enough to be so direct. So you say, "Oh my god, Zack, I'm so sorry, I think I left the oven on in my apartment!" and you run out of the bakery with your bra strap falling down your arm and your purse falling out of your hands.

Relieved to be free of that mess, you set up some dates with guys who seem more stable.

One soft-spoken Guatemalan guy drones on about electronic dance music for two hours straight—apparently he's writing a dissertation about it. Snooze.

Then a goose-pimpled milk-faced wannabe screenwriter doesn't say a single word for ninety minutes. When you finally escape the tapas bar, he grabs your hand and says, "You look like you have really soft lips." Eww!

From that point on you keep dating but stop hoping. It's amazing how many dates you can line up in a single week, even though they are mostly boring and exhausting. And sometimes you DO like a guy (or at least are willing to entertain liking him), and those ones never call you again. You never know why. Romance is a deep and annoying mystery.

A lot of your friends are reading *Fifty Shades of Grey*. You'd prefer a book called *Fifty Shades of Emotional Availability*, in which a normal-looking woman with a normal-looking body falls for a guy who is neither rich nor powerful but just a really decent person. Less handcuffs, more enduring sense of emotional well-being. Probably wouldn't sell.

You're lamenting this to Crystal on the phone one night when she reminds you about that guy *Max412*, the one who spelled things correctly and read Jane Austen. Your original instinct. You decide to message him, and a date is set up. This is officially the first post-Greg date you are really excited about.

Go get him, tiger! Turn to page 49, section 16.

31

You've officially had it with romance, especially online dating. Men look at your profile, then don't message you. Men message you, then don't follow up with an invitation. Men send an invitation, then flake, then text you two weeks later as if nothing happened. If you say anything, *you're* the crazy one. The law of the Internet jungle is that you cannot take anything personally. If you expect reliability or consistency, you are uptight and no fun. The whole thing is a litmus test for how uptight women are and how far you are willing to lower your standards.

You close down all your accounts. *Churlishbutgirlish* is no more. Your first screen name before Greg was *morebeeswithhoney.* Today, after yet another breakup, your screen name would be *ihateyou.* What's the point anyway?

You fall to your knees in a moment of desperation. *Help me,* you whisper. *Please.*

The response is overwhelming: perfect silence.

This is the silence of complete loneliness, loneliness without end. It weighs you down, like your cells are now stones.

You lay down on your couch for a really long time . . .

Turn to page 122, section 35.

32

"Greg!" you gasp.

He looks shockingly . . . human. The man wreaked such havoc on your heart that in your mind he had morphed into a powerful, almost mythic figure. In truth the breakup was more memorable than the actual relationship. Dealing with it, healing from it, has changed you more than the time you spent together. And now here he is—just a guy. Stubbly. Bear-like. Familiar. Your brain feels thick.

"I didn't know if you'd be coming home," he said. "I figured you'd be out with a new boyfriend or something."

"I am. I was. I mean . . . what are you doing here?" you ask. But you know what he's doing here. This is the moment you've dreamed of forever. The moment Greg tells you, "I made a terrible mistake. I'm so sorry, baby. I love you—I think I was having a midlife crisis or something. I'd do anything to get you back. Tell me what to do."

You let him in your apartment, if only to relish this moment. You're still reeling from your evening, and this is an interesting distraction. You both sit on your couch, and you smell his corn chip smell. You let him cry, let him beg. "Oasis was an idiot. You are a goddess . . . " Blah blah blah. Godammit, this should feel more satisfying than it does. Why do they always come back at the precise moment you don't care anymore?

On the other hand, there's symmetry to it. Your recent escapades began with Greg breaking your heart. Shouldn't they end with him mending it? You did always love him. Don't you both deserve a chance at happily ever after?

If you give him another chance,
turn to page 111, section 33.

If you've evolved beyond Greg,
turn to page 201, section 55.

33

Hooray—you got your man back! You always were a big softie, weren't you? And now that Greg lost you once, he suddenly appreciates you in a way he didn't before. At night he squeezes you tight and says he'll never let you go. You fall in love again, now in a less deluded way. The first time around, Greg was God-like in your eyes. Now you see him as far from perfect, but you're okay with it.

One Sunday you're enjoying a day at the beach together when your friend Crystal unexpectedly shows up, wearing a flowing green robe.

"Hey, what are you doing?" you ask, putting down your novel.

"I'm an ordained minister of the Internet Rose Ministries. I've come to marry you to Greg."

"Is it okay, baby?" Greg asks, his milky eyes swimming with tears.

In your childhood there had been images of flowing cream lace dresses, of bridal veils, and daisy bouquets—and drunken speeches made by your parents. Now you're ready to give up the fantasy of the wedding for the reality of simply being married.

So you guys say your vows right then and there, you in your sandy tank top and board shorts, Greg in his damp Speedos.

After that, time moves at an astonishing pace. It's a winding road of negotiations, phone bills, holidays with in-laws, sex, health fads, a mortgage, binge-watching TV shows, less sex, health scares, gray hairs, under-eye cream, wine glasses in the sink, old fights, new fights, *where'd you put my sunglasses* . . . and suddenly it's twenty-five years of marriage later and it all happened so fast.

And tonight all you can tell yourself is that you obviously hadn't planned on killing him.

And to be clear, you never could have actually taken a weapon and sliced right through his flesh, through the valleys of muscles and tendons and right to his bright white bones. Nor would you ever have dreamed of wrapping a gloved hand around a pistol and lodging a bullet into his spleen. No, such acts would have been unthinkable.

But tonight when Greg started choking on his pepper steak, gasping and wheezing and grasping for your hand, well . . . you let him. Not with the cold gaze of a heartless killer either, though that was something the two police officers in your kitchen could never understand. No, it was awful and surreal to watch him die in front of you. But that wouldn't make you any less culpable, so you had to prevaricate a bit.

"You're saying you were in the bathroom when your husband started choking?"

"Yes, sir," you say, looking the clean-shaven cop right in the eye. You sip your tea and don't have to try to look shaken—you are.

"And you couldn't hear anything?" the chubbier cop asks.

"No, of course not," you allow an edge to creep into your tone. You have seen enough television to know that innocent people get defensive when they're accused of something—only the guilty remain calm.

"Do you normally take five or six minutes in the bathroom, Miss?"

Your bathroom is painted yellow with a framed photo of an old Clint Eastwood movie. The bargain had been that you could get scented soaps if Greg could get Clint. There was no bargaining about leaving the toilet seat down—he simply wouldn't do it. He found the request enraging and thought your argument—that all civilized men made this concession for their wives—just reflected how emasculated modern men had become. *More to the point, though,* he explicated one evening over leftover paella—and Lord, Greg loved to explicate—*it's such an inane request, it's so trivial, I can't believe you'd bother to get mad about it.*

This was the way Greg shut down a conversation—by pretending to appeal to your maturity. And it was hard for you to argue that the toilet was a serious matter; you aren't globally insensitive—you know there are bigger problems in the world.

What incensed you was Greg's refusal to understand the symbolism of the issue, how it made you feel neglected, disregarded. How those feelings *were* important in a relationship. He just refused to look at it through your eyes. Several years ago Dr. Cain had said that the key to successful relationships was a rich understanding of the other person's experience. You had heard those words with a sinking heart. You know that for all of Greg's good qualities—and he had many—the ability to truly understand your inner world would never be one of them. He was, however, witty, hardworking, and generally good-natured.

"I'd say my bathroom times vary. On this particular evening I wasn't feeling great."

"How come?" Neither cop is drinking the tea, and the jasmine fragrance steams up from their china cups.

You sigh and pretend to think about it, because answers that spill too quickly sound rehearsed. "I actually wasn't feeling very well that night."

"Why is that, do you think?"

"I think I had some bad chicken for lunch."

The chubby cop is sitting just where Greg had, Greg with his nostril hair and protruding gut. Greg who once dumped you for Oasis. Greg who scored "Low" on the Compassion quiz in *Marie Claire* magazine. What more did you need to know? Greg may have taken out the garbage, washed his own dishes, and ordered in soup when you were sick, but he performed these things with studied dedication, like a dutiful student. He never said, "Aww." He had never once said "Awww."

"Where was that now?"

"At Lil Bits Café on Twelfth Street," you say truthfully, prepared. "I'm sure I have the receipt in my wallet. I was there with my friend Crystal."

"That won't be necessary," clean-shaven cop says. "I'm sorry we have to ask these questions but . . . was everything going okay in your marriage?"

"Yes. Greg and I have . . . had a strong, healthy relationship."

"You seemed to take an awfully long time to call the police."

"I was in shock," you say, and that was true too. You hadn't planned on letting Greg perish. You loved him. At one time you were madly in love with him. It's just that when he started choking, time stilled. You floated out of your body, watched the scene from afar. You both looked old and tired. How many nights had the two of you shared at that kitchen table? How many glasses of wine, heated conversations? Neither of you were yellers, but conversations could be tense. How cold Greg had been at his own father's funeral. What a wreck you had been when he lost his job instead of being supportive. The questions about the girl from the Internet—was it serious? Had they met in person? Why had he been willing to risk everything again? The last question required no answer.

The gradual death of love was insidious but unmistakable. For the past ten years a painful loneliness gripped your insides. You walked around with a sinking feeling in your belly all the time. Once, in the middle of the night, you asked Greg if he ever felt lonely. He hugged you with his strong arms, and said, *Of course not.* You had no idea whether he was intentionally lying or didn't even know how bad things had gotten or maybe he did know but was trying to comfort you. It strikes you now that *his* inner world was a mystery to *you*, not just vice versa. What if all your conclusions and dime-store analyses of him were just wrong? What if the ugly baffling ways he seemed to change were not changes at all but merely projections of your own sadnesses finally coming to the surface? What if he was the same Greg all along—kind, considerate, and dear?

With a wrenching pain, you burst into tears, and this is a good thing because the police are actually beginning to grow suspicious.

"It wasn't perfect!" you cry out. "There was cheating and silent treatments, and he always erased my favorite shows! I can be a real bitch too! But that's marriage! I want him back—you've got to believe me, I want him back!" You sob into your folded arms, regret rolling over you in sickening waves.

"We believe you, ma'am," chubby says, and the two men get

up to go. There is really no reason to think this is anything other than an accident—a poor schlep, and an odd woman who waited one minute too long to call the police. They leave you to your grieving, a project that will never complete.

You sit at the table for hours, even when dusk gives into blackness. You sit upright only once, when a terrible thought occurs to you. *We should have had a child.*

You sit like that until morning. Then you get up to make a fresh cup of tea.

THE END

34

Your heart roars as you whisper *Fuck fuck fuck.* Thank God you brought your purse! You apply pressed powder to your upper lip and chin to conceal the redness from Steve's stubble and then reapply your lipstick once more. (Why oh why did you pick a lipstick color called *Brazen*?) It still doesn't look great but you're terrified of bumping into Steve again, so you run back into the dining room. Your vision blurs with tears.

"Are you okay?" J. P. asks.

"Yes, yes," you whisper in his ear. "I'm just drunk."

J. P. believes you because he is a sweet and wonderful person, and you are a disgusting moral reprobate.

It's time for almond tart and strawberries with cream, and your only goal is to avoid having a complete nervous breakdown. What the hell were you thinking? Why were you willing to endanger the one amazing relationship you've had in years? Are you afraid to be happy?

You love J. P.! No—you are desperately in love with him!

No—that's crazy too! How can you be desperately in love with someone you've known for only three months?

Ahh! What is love? What the hell is love anyway? What are you? What is life?

"So can you get your brother a job?" Mr. Moretti is asking J. P.

"Don't waste your breath," Steve says. "J. P. doesn't want a slacker like me at Spoiled Geniuses Incorporated."

"That has nothing to do with family!" Mr. Moretti yells, but not particularly at J. P. It seems like he just wants to make a big declaration.

"Dad," J. P. says calmly. "Steve has never even taken the LSAT."

"Well, then, it is what it is," Mother says, her bird-like face placid. "HE'LL HAVE TO FIND SOMETHING ELSE!"

J. P. squeezes your hand under the table. You want to lick his fingers, like the dog that you are. Instead, you just squeeze back. The rest of the night you don't let go.

THE END

121

35

The first months without dating are brutal. The practice had been as much a way to fill time as it was a romantic endeavor. The whole online scene had a manic feeling to it. One minute you were rejected, the next you were buzzing with activity. Now life has flat-lined. Everyone else is behind closed doors with their puppies and tricycles and inspirational quotes on the refrigerator. Behind your closed door is just . . . you. You have tried and failed to find a partner. Now you have to find a way to make your life bearable.

This is a difficult mission. You can't do something crazy like quit your job and join an ashram because there is this thing called money and another thing called health insurance. And you can't become a mountain climber or a daredevil because you've got a bum knee. So what you must do is figure out what, besides men, really makes you happy in life. And it's amazing to see how little you know about this.

You start singing in the shower, mostly folk songs.

You join a knitting club from Meetup.org.

You take motorcycle lessons.

You write a children's book called *Puppies and Peanut Butter* about a puppy who keeps getting peanut butter stuck to the roof of his mouth. It's stupid and you never find a publisher, but it's a very fun experience.

You go to your friends' houses—the ones who have kids—but this time without the resentment. Some are pretty cute, with cheeks like plump, juicy peaches.

You go to the movies by yourself. You see everything. You post your snarky comments on Facebook. One time you get seventy likes.

You read everything by Joyce Carol Oates. This takes a while.

You pray. You don't pray for things to change; you pray to be open to lightness and joy. You don't pray to a god in the sky. You pray to lightness itself, joy itself. You ask them if they'll touch you. Sometimes they do. Sometimes they don't.

It's not that you get happy, but you get busy. You stop pushing against the tide. You're okay. Not amazing, but okay. You get to the point where you honestly don't care about meeting a man.

Which is precisely, of course, when you meet Anthony. Well, you don't exactly meet him—he's here to fix your toilet.

"Do you see the problem?" you ask him, hovering uncomfortably by the bathroom door. You're sure you use too much toilet paper, and many previous plumbers have shamed you for it. You await your scolding.

"Yeah, don't worry about it. I'll be done in a few."

Well, that's nice. Anthony has a terrific New York accent,

which you always enjoy. He's got thick, arched brows, like he's daring you. And somehow he's conquered the whole plumber ass-crack problem. He wears tight jeans, but they stay in place. Wait—are you checking out a plumber's ass?

Reminding yourself that this isn't a Leonard Melfi play, you return to the living room, where you are working on your home computer. There is much to be said about the distinctions between green teas: the crisp rice flavor of genmaicha versus the pungent floral jasmine versus the sweet refreshing Japanese sencha. Los Angeles may be the only place in the world that wants to hear about this, but when *Downward Dogs* yoga magazine asks you to write an article, who are you to say no?

"All done here, miss," Anthony says. The word *miss* makes you feel grown up, even though you are wearing your college sweatpants and an old tank top.

"Oh thanks! Do you want some water or something?"

"Sure, that'd be great. Cute apartment. I like the picture over your toilet," he says, referring to your framed *Ghostbusters* poster.

"Oh, thanks," you say. You're not exactly embarrassed; after all, *Ghostbusters* is one of the finest films ever made. But something about Tony's gleaming arms and the hair poking out of his V-neck makes you self-conscious.

"Sometimes I feel like people don't talk enough about Egon," you say, referring to the nerdiest of the busters.

"Oh yeah, I agree," Anthony says. He has a very full mouth and olive skin. "I mean, Egon is really the brains behind the whole operation."

You laugh and open the refrigerator for a pitcher of water. (You keep one handy in case the faucets go dry. Why aren't more people panicking about the drought?)

"I also have iced green tea if you like," you offer.

"Oh, sure, that sounds good. Antioxidants and whatnot, right?"

"Right!"

Somehow you're shaky as you reach for a glass. You can't remember the last time a man was in your apartment, let alone one who is swarthy and sweating. The sudden rush of masculine energy shifts the climate, like when a plane experiences a change in cabin pressure. The glass falls right out of your hand and shatters on the kitchen floor.

Pull your shit together, girl! Continue to page 129, section 36.

36

"Oh shit, I'm sorry!" You curse yourself as you kneel on the floor to scoop up the shards.

"No, no, you're barefoot. Get outta here," Anthony says. "Where's a broom?"

It's not like a broken glass is a ticking nuclear bomb, but somehow Anthony seems like an action-movie hero.

You pad out of the kitchen after handing him a broom. He sweeps up the mess and finds two glasses. They probably have spots on them! (Why can't you be as immaculate as your friend Meg?) Now he's pouring both of you iced sencha tea.

"Thanks so much," you say, wishing you weren't wearing a stained ribbed tank, circa 1992. There is no elastic left. For all Anthony knows, you are shapeless. "Have a seat."

The two of you chit-chat for a bit—how long have you lived here, traffic is crazy, and so forth. Soon Anthony's easy-going manner relaxes you.

"How'd you get into plumbing anyway?" you ask, for it's one of the last jobs on earth you would ever consider.

"Well, I'm not squeamish," Anthony says with a smile. It's like he can tell that *you* are. "And it's a job that has actual stability in this economy. It seemed like a smart thing to do."

"Good point," you say, not sure if these are good enough reasons to work with toilets and shimmy under houses.

"Yeah—money's good. I was able to put a down payment on a place in Culver City," he says.

You snob! You scribble haikus about cheese puffs for chump change; Anthony actually has a stable job and a house in a great area. You feel yourself blush.

Anthony rescues you with a surprising offer: "Maybe you want to see it sometime. There's a funky little bar right near me. Only place in town with genuine New York–style pizza."

"Oh!" you say, blushing again. (Weren't you supposed to outgrow blushing in your teens?) "So you're not married, I take it?"

"I was," Anthony says. "We were high school sweethearts. It was a long time ago. She's a terrific lady."

Oooh, the positive report about an ex—always a good sign!

Your heart is beating in an undeniable attraction to Anthony (and his accent). But there is an unfamiliar feeling mingling with the excitement. It's . . . it's . . . it's a quiet stillness. It's a *lack of desperation*. You like your life right now. That gaping void has been filled with actual confidence and a bit of acceptance for whatever life brings. You'd really like to go to Anthony's, but it's not like you'll die if you don't.

And now that you realize how mature you've become, you attack Anthony like a frenzied Koala bear freed from captivity.

You kiss his hot, beautiful mouth and squeeze those glistening hairy arms. You want to rip off your ugly tank top, but Anthony slows you down with a smoldering slowness that drives you crazy. He lets his fingers graze around your waist and your rib cage. He pulls you close to him and kisses you deeply. He won't go too far. His masculinity pulses off him in thick, hot waves. You want to ride him like a Harley. He won't let you, which is hotter than anything. And why? *He wants to take you on a proper date.* Is this guy for real?

"Okay," you say with a smile. If the universe wants you to fall in love with your sexy New York plumber, who are you to disobey?

Turns out, that's exactly what the universe wants. And it turns out, over time, that Anthony is not just some sexy Stanley Kowalski; he's a real person. He reads Malcolm Gladwell. He cooks and cleans. He has restless leg syndrome.

And he's still the best kisser you ever met. When Anthony kisses you with that full, hot mouth, you enter a dream state. It's like he's speaking to you with his lips. It's like his lips are saying, "I love you, baby."

"I love you, baby," his lips actually say one day, and you pour your face onto his hairy chest and kiss it tenderly. Then you say it back. One must always wait for the guy to say it first!

He's not the person you expected to fall for, but you're noticing that the less you analyze stuff, the happier you are. In this way *you're* different from what you expected. Or maybe it's the same you, but a person is a like a planet spinning around the sun. Every new situation sheds sunlight on a different part of you, and it's a different time and season in different parts of your world all at the same moment. This is the season of you and Anthony. You don't believe in the idea of The One, but you believe in Anthony and he believes in you. Nothing has ever felt more right.

It happens like this, guys, you tell your friends, the married ones who are divorcing now. The ones you used to be so jealous of. You don't feel triumphant; you honestly want them to be as happy as you are. *It will get better*, you tell them. *Just don't give up on giving up.*

THE END

37

Slow down, sister! First, you're ready to become America's next heiress with Jun, then the Great White Hope in Haiti, and all of it for romantic love?! What is wrong with you?

Answer: You are too concerned with men. Period. You can't uproot your whole life just to follow a swell guy. You tell Amad you're not ready to take that leap. He understands, of course, because he is the best thing since sliced bread.

And speaking of bread . . . uhm, remember your career? Your life as a food critic? The term "slacking off" is putting your recent work life mildly. If it weren't for rent control, you'd be in big trouble. And the truth is, food *is* your passion. Not just its lusciousness but also the way people relate to it, use it to express love and care, or hide themselves in it. Especially desserts. It seems each one performs a different emotional function. The soothing comfort of bread pudding. The heady intoxication of a dark chocolate brownie. The nostalgic innocence of a chocolate chip cookie.

"Then do something about it!" Meg Skypes you one night.

"What do you want me to do about cookies?" you ask. "I already critique them."

"Something more," she says. "Shit, the baby is screaming."

This is the way most conversations with your parent friends

end, always before you're done talking. It's one of the many reasons you need cookies. What desserts does a haggard parent need, though? Or, for that matter, an astronaut? Or a social worker?

Your curiosity leads you to a brainstorm. You will interview women about their relationship with desserts. You will make a book or documentary or web series—you don't know yet, but it's a project!

You throw yourself in with abandon. You stay up nights researching the history of the honey-cake. You talk to psychologists and neurologists about the chemicals released by eating sugar and butter. You interview women across the economic and cultural spectrum about their relationship with sweets. You make friends and learn a ton. You feel energized again. You feel alive and connected. Forget romance—you are participating in life! The space in your brain once occupied by men is now crammed with the psychology of Bundt cake and the creation of sweet jelabi in Iraq in 300 BC, which ancient Iraqis claimed had a mystical power.

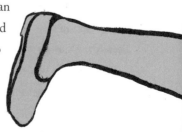

You'd like to discuss this with an up-and-coming pastry chef named Jeremy, who has brought jelabi to the United States. You're speaking with him in the kitchen of the new

restaurant he cooks for. You're a little heady from the smell of spun sugar but try to focus on your interview. "What made you connect with Indian desserts?" you ask him.

Jeremy hands you a bright orange swirl of jelabi, and you take a bite, immediately suffused by its sweetness. Jelabi, a deep-fried flour pretzel covered in sugar syrup, is heavenly and instantly addictive.

"Whoa," you say.

"You like it?" Jeremy asks. He has a gentle open face, a mound of baldness on his head, and a mound of pudge on his belly.

He hands you another creation, this one a double-chocolate cupcake with peanut butter filling.

"You've got frosting on your lip," he points out.

"Fohfskj," you say, your cheeks stuffed with peanut butter.

Then there's an apple pie bar (and witty banter with Jeremy).

Then poppy seed cake with passion-fruit curd (Jeremy is a widower with a son who means the world to him).

Then a cherry square drizzled with Nutella (Jeremy loves *Jane Eyre* as much as you and totally gets that *Moby Dick* is a drag).

Then there's a pumpkin chocolate-chip muffin and you shoving Jeremy down on the kitchen counter in a wild paroxysm of lust. You kiss him hungrily, bite his neck, claw your hands down his back. You sink your teeth into his love handles.

Whatever chemicals desserts unleash (oxytocin? serotonin?),

they've combined to send a cupid's arrow into your heart, revealing Jeremy to be as scrumptious as his strawberry rhubarb meringue tartlet.

In the years that follow, Jeremy will support you as you become a food documentarian, and he will challenge you to stay focused and thriving. In return you will generously sample all his pastries and help raise his sensitive and eccentric son.

It's not perfect, of course. Jeremy definitely has a weight problem, his son has agoraphobia, and you may or may not have fibromyalgia.

But you once heard a saying that "perfect is the enemy of good." And this new life is pretty darn good. In the mornings Jeremy kisses your face and calls you his little jelabi. It's the best thing ever.

Who knew life as a fried pretzel could be so sweet?

THE END

38

Some people wake up at five in the morning so they can hit the gym before work. Others simply find time to lift weights or go to Pilates at some point during the week. They claim it improves their mood. All of these people are incomprehensible to you. How can people *choose* the gym when there is Candy Crush, talking on the phone, and snacks? Sure, you'd love to look like the gals on the billboards—mostly so you could never have to worry about it again. But without a DNA overhaul, that ain't gonna happen, so why not enjoy life instead of spending it in a dungeon sweating?

That was your old philosophy anyway. After the underwear fiasco, things look different. You still hate exercise, but now you are on a mission. You join the Malibu Bikini Beach Body Competition for one reason only: to make Greg rue the day he left you.

Your first trainer is named Tiffany, and she works mostly with chunky members of the local Armenian community who rave about her on Yelp. They probably love her because she looks like an exotic alien. Spray-tanned, sinewy, and blonde is a trustworthy look for a personal trainer. Who cares that her blog, *Tighten Up with Tiffany!*, is riddled with spelling errors? In your free "consultation session" Tiffany tells you straight: "You're not in the worst shape in the world, but bikini-beach-body ready is a whole other level."

"What do you mean?" you mumble. People like Tiffany make you uncomfortable. You feel both superior and piteously inadequate at the same time.

"It means you'll have to borderline starve yourself—eating only egg whites, steamed veggies, and water for eight weeks straight until the competition."

Whoa whoa whoa—this can't be the only way. "That seems a little dramatic," you say.

"It is. Are you in?"

"I'd like to think about it," you say, knowing you will never call Tiffany again. A part of you finds her fascist regime appealing, as it offers the promise of a Brand-New You. It's also horrifying.

Many trainers are already booked up, so you settle for a fortysomething Frenchman named Claude, a chubby cherub whose protruding gut does not exactly scream fitness. Apparently he had been at the top of his game back in the day, so you decide to give it a whirl. You're allowed to eat more than veggies with Claude, but he does start you on a grueling routine of crunches, weight lifting, and core strengtheners. Claude designs excellent sequences, even if he himself could not endure them, and while you lay huffing and puffing on your towel afterward, he chats with you.

"That ex-boyfriend of yours must be some kind of idiot," he says on your first day in a kind way that does not creep you out. He has a beaming face and a wonderful French accent.

"I'm the idiot," you say. "I'm not great at reading signs."

"Maybe you're just loyal," Claude says.

"Well, yeah, but . . . well, yeah!" It's nice not to feel judged for a minute. Or maybe you're too tired to argue.

The next day you're sore as hell, but Claude is merciless, which you appreciate.

"I want Greg to see that those airbrushed airheads have got nothing on me," you say as you pull down on the weight machine.

"Does Greg like airbrushed airheads?"

You remember Oasis, who probably thinks Axelrod is the name of a new dildo instead of a political strategist. "Doesn't everyone?" you laugh, with a drop of bitterness.

"Well, no," Claude says. "Some men like someone they can actually talk to. And who was it that said a woman's beauty is the light in her heart . . ."

"Hmmph," you say, wanting to believe him. Most of your friends put considerable time and energy into looking their best. Part of you wants to do that too, but, as you tell Claude, "Part of me is still stuck on the old-fashioned notion that someone could love me for me."

"I think that's the point," Claude says. As a widowed father of a young daughter, he doesn't like the way you put yourself down. He says you could probably be a lot easier on yourself.

Claude starts bringing you his favorite comic books—collections of *Calvin and Hobbes*. He says you need to laugh more. It's a funny coincidence because you used to love those books as a kid. Okay, so Claude doesn't read Kafka like Greg did, but Hobbes is a damned profound stuffed tiger.

"Greg would go nuts if he saw my quads right now," you say one day over butt squeezes. "The man was obsessed with thighs."

"You still carry a torch, *oui?*"

You squirt water into your mouth for a moment of rest. "Not exactly. We were together for a few years. He was so smart and witty. I guess I always felt that if I could keep Greg's attention, then I must really have something. But I never could. Greg could barely sit still with me for more than ten minutes."

Claude just nods in his gentle way and instructs you to do some more calf raises. By week three he comments on how hungry and irritable you are. He says you're making the bikini contest too important. You grunt, but his concern touches you.

In fact, you are so depleted that you don't notice when Claude starts lightening the exercise load or sneaking full-fat yogurt and peanut butter into your protein shakes. Your talks grow longer, and one time you go out to lunch with Claude and his little daughter, Amy, and you two like each other instantly. When Amy creeps up to you for a good-bye hug, you almost burst into tears.

The next day Amy sends Claude with a bunch of fresh-baked chocolate chip cookies for you—the perfect gooey texture with hints of vanilla. You can't resist eating all of them. And when Claude moves in to kiss the crumbs off your lips, you can't resist that either. Your first kiss is just like a cookie: sweet, warm, and oddly nostalgic.

By week five, training has been replaced completely with fun walks on the beach (sometimes with Amy), cookie eating, and making out. You can't remember the last time a guy made out with you without trying to get you naked. It could be insulting, but the long hours of kissing on the couch feel amazing. No, Claude doesn't have a razor-sharp wit like Greg, but you're beginning to forget why that felt important. Plus, he's very rugged and adventurous, which makes you feel safe. He likes kayaking and windsurfing and hiking in dangerous places. Not like you want to do any of that stuff, but you like the way Claude's face lights up when he talks about things he's passionate about. His face also lights up when he tells you how much he likes you.

By week eight and the day of the contest you are officially chubby, unqualified, and happy for the first time in months. You don't even notice what day it is as you and Claude snuggle on the couch and watch movies in the middle of the afternoon while munching herb popcorn and mint-chip ice cream.

You learn later that your absence leaves witty Greg wandering the beach alone—scanning the parade of taut, glistening women for the only one he stood a chance with, the one he had taken miserably for granted just for being exactly who you are. He slumps home with a sunburn on his nose and an ache in his chest.

That evening he texts you at last: *I made a big mistake.* ☹ *Please take me back. I love you so much.*

If you know Greg has always been your true love, turn to page 111, section 33.

If you've evolved beyond Greg and want to try things with Claude, turn to page 55, section 17.

39

"Argh!" you scream this time while you push, a technique you've seen Amy use when she's kicking a soccer ball. Now there is a little give, but not enough to help groaning Claude. You take a deep breath and wipe the sweat off your forehead. The pressure stings where the asphalt scraped you raw. You look down at Claude, whose eyes are wide.

"Don't worry," you say with the steady certainty of a Navy SEAL—or your mother.

And now you summon every bit of strength in your little body, every muscle straining and contracting, every cell joining in the effort. The tendons in your neck bulge. And you push the trunk with enough force that Claude can roll away and lie flat on his back. You put your hands on your knees and recover your breath. You're amazing!

"I think I slipped a disc," Claude says, though he doesn't actually know what that means.

The neighborhood stays outside for a while, wary of aftershocks. The lights are out, but since no one is seriously injured and all the pets have been found, people can be nice to each other again. A smattering of hugs, a few pats on the back. Amy sings a little song she has made up.

Someone suggests s'mores and a sing-a-long, which gets a few laughs, but no one is going to get *that* community. There are tweets to tweet, pictures to upload. People return to their homes and light candles, have a drink, argue, or get naked.

After you tuck Amy back in, you help Claude into bed and give him three ibuprofen to wash down with scotch.

"You're my hero," he says softly.

"You were pretty scared there," you reply with kindness.

"Yeah. I was." Turns out when it happens, Claude *isn't* scared to admit it. And that's all the turn-on you need.

You blow out the candle.

THE END

40

You push through the crowd and find a tall muscular woman you think can help. Her name is Annie, and she leaps into action, running back with you. But by the time you two reach Claude, he's managed to get himself free.

"I'm okay, *belle-fille*," he says. He's holding Amy's hand and limping a bit.

All of a sudden you're scared you've gotten in way too deep.

Sure, Claude helped you through a tough time (when you temporarily lost your mind and decided to become a beach bunny), but that doesn't mean he's the right guy for you. If you've learned anything from Greg, it's that you need to slow down and think things through.

You'll wait to tell Claude until he's recovered from his back injury.

That night he falls asleep quickly after downing some ibuprofen with whiskey. Amy goes down hard too—no whiskey required.

At 3 a.m. you're almost ready to crawl into bed, but after the fall and the alcohol, Claude's snoring is downright astonishing. He sounds like a plane taking off, poor dear. You decide to sit on the curb and take in the moonlight. Looks like Annie had the same idea.

She's got a thermos full of vodka, and why not? The night is weird enough as is.

The next four hours fly by. Annie is hilarious and loves to hear the tales of your romantic adventures with men. Turns out her adventures with women are all too similar. You're thinking it's pretty cool how tonight's disaster might bring you a new friend when suddenly Annie kisses you gently on the mouth.

"Oh," you say, surprised.

"I'm sorry," she blushes. "I always crush on straight girls."

"It's okay . . . I'm just . . . yeah, straight."

"Can we still be friends?" she asks.

"Of course!" you say. Gay or straight, Annie may be your only single friend left. And now that you've made a mental decision about Claude, it will be great to have a gal pal to go out with and nurse your blues.

You're eating shredded wheat with Claude a week later when he beats you to the punch.

"You're not happy, huh?" he asks gently.

You're surprised he noticed. So often in a breakup it seems like the two people have been living in two different realities, albeit within the same relationship.

"I guess not," you falter, and you didn't expect the lump in your throat to rise so quickly. After all, you had this idea two weeks ago. But you've grown attached to Claude, and the thought of being on your own again fills you with terrible dread. You're sick of the hunt. You're sick of breaking up. You're sick of everything.

"I know how you feel," Annie says. You're back in your apartment, having moved all your clothes from Claude's place. Claude's little beach house was so breezy and uncluttered. Your place is a stuffy, chaotic pigsty. Annie says she'll help you get more organized.

She's a very responsible person, an accountant who is used to doing things perfectly. Everything except love, that is. It's such a relief to talk to Annie. As much as you have often craved male attention, it's really women who understand you. And isn't that what it's really about? You entertain a brief fantasy about living with Annie—how you could talk about feelings and laugh at the same things. How you would feel seen and would see her too. How no one would leave the toilet seat up.

You've got your head on her shoulders and her arm is wrapped around you.

Your heart is pounding.

Should you go for it?

If you're ready to enter a Sapphic state of bliss, turn to page 152, section 42.

If you feel a little old to switch sexual orientations, turn to page 154, section 43.

41

You and Artie read books after playtime, books where little boys and girls cooperate and make mistakes and learn lessons and love their mommies. You even read *Goodnight Zoo* even though it's daytime. Night night, lions. Night night, shark.

Max texts at 6:30.

Leaving soon—I should be home for tubby time. ☺

That's unusual, lately. Does he know you know? You don't want to do tubby time with him. You can't play nice in front of Artie. You might actually lose your mind if you have to do that. So you run the water now. Tubby time will happen earlier tonight. Artie kicks and screams over this, but it's just too bad. You promise you'll give him cookies if he'll just get in the tub, so he does. Maybe this is bad parenting, but what can you do? You quickly soap him up, skip washing his hair, put him in his giraffe pajamas, give him cookies, and let him watch *Sesame Street* on the iPad until he mercifully falls asleep. It's eight o'clock by this time anyway, so Max's text was another lie.

Now you are sitting on the couch, still in your robe, and it's eight-fifteen when Max comes through the door. He moves quietly in case Artie is sleeping, which is just the sort of thing you always thought meant he was so sensitive. Now what does it mean?

There are speeches to deliver, tears to shed, plates to shatter across the kitchen. But you are too tired for this or don't know how to do it. You just sigh and say shakily, "I saw the pictures."

Max is thin with warm hazel eyes. Max is Artie's father. Max has his Max smell, but now Max is a mystery.

Do you give him credit for not trying to deny anything? He stands there frozen for a second, then runs over to you and drops to his knees. He is tearful, apologetic. He admits he was selfish and self-centered and an imbecile. Supposedly that's what you'd want to hear, but the words don't really land, just as none of this quite has, despite the hot stabbing painful fingers gripping your organs.

It's true, it's true, it's true—I'm not enough. And I'll always hate him for making me remember that. You sit there, frozen but ill. Max asks if he should sleep on the couch tonight. You say the truth: *I don't know anything. I don't know.*

What happens from this point on will be a matter of science. Brains adapt to new information and create new schemas to accommodate them. Your old brain knew Max to be someone who wouldn't pulverize your heart. Now your brain has to incorporate Lying Cheating Max into the new schema, which could spoil the whole thing, destroy the neural pathway that associates Max with love, comfort, and security. Or, perhaps if Max demonstrates renewed commitment and convinces you, you can adjust to a third Max, neither the old Max nor the new dangerous Max but some other Max who you could love and mostly trust, provided he loves the new you.

You hope for the best, but in the end it's up to your brain.

THE END

42

"Annie . . . " you whisper, and suddenly Annie envelops you in a deep and tender kiss. You let it unfold, kiss her back, let her caress you. You want to discover if you can surrender to this. Turns out . . .

You can! Annie's hand on your back makes your stomach flutter. Annie's kiss makes you feel light, like you're flying. When Annie takes you into her arms, you feel an aching tenderness. You feel yourself turning toward her, like an orchid toward the sun.

Who knew? All this time women could have been an option? You'll be damned!

Or maybe it's just that Annie is the right person at the right time. From this night onward you spend every minute together. You chitter and chatter all night long and talk or text incessantly throughout the day. At night you explore each other's bodies with the fevered curiosity of naked scientists.

One night you take her to an artisanal ice cream shop that has just opened. You order pepper-peach and she gets coconut curry, but you keep swirling them together to make even more strange and delicious combinations. You look at Annie, her tan skin, and witty hazel eyes. You keep trying to figure out if it's her femininity or masculinity that attracts you, but the question is a puzzle

puzzle leading nowhere. It's just her *Annie*-ness.

And it's more proof that the best things in life are completely unpredictable.

THE END

43

For the love of God, woman—stop being so reckless with people! First Claude, now Annie? Every time you need an ego-boost you jump into a relationship with someone? You're worse than Greg!

"I'm sorry, Annie," you say lovingly. "I can't."

"I totally get it," she says. "We're both fucked up, huh?" She kisses your forehead on the way out your door.

Alone again in your humid cave, you have to admit she's right. You pick up a bottle of white wine but then put it back in the refrigerator. You turn on the television but then turn it off immediately. Forlorn, you sit there blankly. Then a voice inside says, *It's time to start facing reality and grow up.*

"Shut up," you say back and pop a peanut butter cup in your mouth.

No, really, the voice says. *Stop turning your back on yourself.*

The voice is firm but gentle. You decide to listen to it.

Taking care of yourself begins with the obvious: eating more leafy greens and taking walks in the sunshine. The annoying part is that those things do help. You start reading more and lay off scanning Facebook for all the ways you are inferior to your "friends." You stop beating yourself up mentally and find that, surprisingly, self-kindness is actually more motivating than constant criticism.

You rededicate yourself to working hard at your job. You even get a weekly column called *Tough Cookie* in an online food magazine. As is the way when you put yourself out there, opportunities beget more opportunities. You are hired to teach a course called Food in Literature at a junior college. You get to pore over your favorite passages from *Like Water for Chocolate* and *The Edible Woman*. Someone thinks you should even do a TED talk. Your friendships with Crystal, Meg, and Annie are wonderful.

Things are going well, so why is there this pit in your stomach all the time? It's not just loneliness; loneliness is familiar and you're not afraid of it anymore. It's more than that. You go over your recent romantic history in your head, seeking loose ends.

Greg: Dumped you, probably for the best. Check.

Pad thai delivery guy: Greedy for chicken, not relationship material. Check.

Claude: You loved him but got very scared. Check.

Annie: Amazing, but you're not a lesbian. Check.

Wait—back up. What was that about Claude again? Your stomach twists in horror. You were in a beautiful relationship with a caring, sexy Frenchman, and you ran off as soon as it started to feel real. What is wrong with you? It wasn't Claude who couldn't admit to fear—it was you! You love Claude! Ahhhh!

In the movies it's usually the man who realizes that he was

just scared of commitment and starts running to his lady's door. In *your* movie, *you're* the commitment-phobic dummy, and the "running" is a ninety-minute drive in merciless traffic to Claude's tiny Venice beach house. And he's not home. And you're an idiot. Again.

It's going to be a long drive back, and you need to stretch your legs first. You try to tell yourself at least you tried, but it's not enough. Your heart is not satisfied now that you are awake to it. And you miss Amy—Jesus, what you'd give to scoop her up and kiss her face.

You trudge along the boardwalk, oblivious to the fire-eaters and tattoo artists. You can't feel the sunshine nor smell the saltwater, body odor, and cotton candy. You know where this is going—the numb ache spreading through your body like hot Novocain. The stomachache that won't quit. The searing violence of another broken heart.

You're so caught up in your impending nightmare that you're blind to the pudgy cherubic father walking with his daughter until he calls out, "*Belle-fille?*"

"Claude!" you shout and run over to him.

For a moment you stand there silently, his eyes tender, your eyes blinded with tears. Then you kiss his darling French lips.

It's the happiest kiss of your life—even better than when the coolest guy in high school kissed you on a dare.

Now Amy tugs at his shirt to get into a group hug.

"Can you ever forgive me?" you ask, eyes swimming with tears.

"Do you want some cotton candy?" Amy asks.

You break a fluff off Amy's pale blue cotton candy and let it evaporate on your tongue. Little crystals remain there, tingling. The taste is as achingly sweet as the man you almost let slip away.

"*Je t'aime*," Claude says, pulling you in tight. "*Je t'aime*."

You don't speak French yet, but you do know what that means. It means he loves you too.

THE END

44

"Tell me what you want," Benjamin whispers in your ear, then licks it.

"You mean say something dirty?" you stall.

"Yeah, that's a good girl."

"I want . . ."

"Yeah, baby?"

"I want your cock out of my pussy right now!" you splutter and tears spring to your eyes.

"Jesus," Benjamin says and removes himself briskly. He rolls the condom off and storms to the bathroom. "What a spaz," he adds.

Maybe you should feel guilty or angry, but you just feel stupid. Benjamin is not great. Benjamin is a total player and you know it. You've been kidding yourself because you wanted to skip the part of the breakup where you really have to be on your own for a while. On the drive home you decide it's time to just pay attention to yourself.

You embark on a mission to get positive. You start doing yoga and try to look for one moment of joy each day, just as an online self-help book recommended. You increase healthy foods like flax and tempeh. You listen to a meditation tape, although

when you are supposed to inwardly chant "may the entire world know love and peace" you find yourself accidentally chanting, "the entire world has a disease."

You seek a positive outlook in the autobiography *Man's Search for Meaning* by Victor Frankl, a sort of pick-me-up-book about the Holocaust. Frankl basically says that Holocaust survivors were people who held on to their optimism and sense of purpose. So you know you would have died in, like, two days.

Ugh, maybe you should write your own book in response to Frankl. Instead of *Man's Search for Meaning*, it will be called *Obviously Life Has No Meaning.*

Your perfectly together friend Meg says you should write it— maybe sublimating your grief through art will illuminate something. Meg signs you up for a local fiction writing class, and who are you to argue?

Class meets at the teacher's apartment, where you sit on overstuffed couches, eat fresh-baked pie and raw cashews, and comment on each other's stories. You have poured out all your feelings about Greg into a story and read it aloud to less than critical acclaim.

"I don't understand why he'd leave her," a girl with bangs says. "It sounds like they had a great relationship."

"Yes!" you say excitedly. "It doesn't make any sense."

"But writing has to make sense," the girl says.

"Oh," you say.

The second class you write about how a breakup is like a death and how Greg murdered your soul. The one cute guy in class looks frightened. He's Indian, and his writing is beautiful and concerned with bigger ideas than your Greg treatise. Stuff like political corruption and the whole Pakistan nuclear bomb thing.

"Jesus, your character is maudlin," he says. "No wonder he left her—the protagonist is so irritating."

"Oh," you say.

In the third class the girl with bangs says, "We need to know more about the protagonist's backstory. Obviously her boyfriend is just a symbol."

You nod politely but really don't want to hear about symbols. You are a food critic, not Virginia Woolf. You want to write about plum sauce.

Maybe you need a different project other than waiting for Greg to have the Big Realization. In the movies men *always* have the Big Realization. Even men who die come back as a ghost to tell you it was a mistake. Even in a movie called *He's Just Not That into You* the guy comes back at the end to say that, as a matter of fact, *he's into you!* There's no movie where you have this great relationship that means everything to you and the guy dumps you and then just never regrets it. No one wants to see that.

You sit at your computer and try to get back to your article about how there's no such thing as too much cilantro—which is funny because you never even buy cilantro at the grocery store. In fact, you never buy anything at the grocery store except bananas and cereal. It's kind of ridiculous that you study food for a living but can't cook! Luckily Groupon has an answer for this: a six-week cooking class where you get to drink wine as you learn. This has got to be the universe offering you the perfect new hobby.

The first class you get drunk and burn your mini pizza.

The second and third classes you make a mediocre radicchio salad and a pesto pasta that's as bitter and oily as you feel.

On class four you try to talk to an older man but he is married. He's one of those married guys who doesn't wear a ring. Gross. You do *not* give him a bite of your (perfectly adequate) tagine.

On class five you've got flour on your nose and an apricot tartlet in the oven when a new guy in glasses enters the room, apologetic and definitely adorable. Your teacher guides him to the table near you and suddenly you recognize him from the Internet: It's *Max412*! The super-cute guy who reads Jane Austen! Max recognizes you too, and when you share a bite of your dessert, he sheepishly asks if you'd like to go on a date.

You take a deep breath and say yes!

**Let's hope he's halfway normal.
Turn to page 49, section 16.**

45

"Seriously, thanks for listening," Zack says again.

"Maybe I'm done listening," you say coyly and slink toward the bathroom. When Zack just sits there, you motion him to come in with you. Your heart is pounding wildly.

And suddenly Zack has slipped into the bathroom, and you charge him like a Spanish bull. It's all deep kissing and him grabbing your hair and sliding his hand under your skirt and you breathing deeply into his neck.

"God, you're hot," he whispers, and somehow suddenly he's sitting on the edge of the bathroom sink and you're sucking away like his impressive organ is a cherry popsicle on a hot summer day.

This is the sluttiest, hottest thing you've ever done (besides college, and who counts college?). It's all over so quickly, and on your way out of the bathroom you can barely make eye contact with him as you yank your skirt back in place.

You drive home knowing you'll never see him again and pretend that's okay with you. So when you get a text the next evening—*I need to see you again*—your heart practically bursts out of your chest. Then he texts you his address, not even awaiting your reply.

You'd just taken your first bite of a roasted turkey sandwich at your kitchen table, but you throw your fork down and head straight over to his downtown loft. You can't remember if you've even shaven your legs, but you don't care. You don't care that his apartment stinks of cigarettes and looks like a cyclone hit it. You need to be in his bed, in his arms, feeling his weight on you as he devours you, you gasping, arching, melting into him.

It's like your skin is on fire and only Zack's touch can cool it down. You feel Zack in every one of your cells.

Days go by like this—the two of you holed up in his apartment, drinking vodka right out of the bottle and fucking like mangy beasts. Occasionally you get up to eat cold mac and cheese. It's disgusting and incredible.

After two weeks, Zack says, it's time to go out!

You taxi to a packed nightclub where sweaty twentysomethings with pierced tongues and spacey eyes grind against each other. You're the oldest people there, but somehow you don't care. You don't care about anything when you're with Zack. You don't care that he wants to snort blow off your sternum in the stinky bathroom. You just want to be near him.

High on coke, Zack is even more energized. He pulls you to the dance floor where you jerk and twist maniacally for half an hour, then Zack needs more coke. He seems to know all the right people, and you never even see money exchange hands.

Then back to the dance floor. Then back for more coke. Then finally you head home and collapse into a crumpled naked heap with him. Limbs intertwined. His mouth on your damp shoulder.

Although you yourself abstained from the hard stuff, you feel you've been on the same wild ride as Zack. The difference is your addiction is to him.

Six weeks go by in a vodka- and lust-soaked blur. You haven't even been to your apartment except to pick up a bunch of clothes and a toothbrush. Mostly you wear clothes that various lovers have left at Zack's—mesh shirts, leather pants, baggy vintage tees. Much of it doesn't fit you, but you don't care. You want to be Zack's bad girl. Your mother is leaving worried texts. Your magazines are wondering where your latest submissions are. And all you can think of is Zack's body pressed against yours, Zack's intoxicating smell, Zack's hands on your aching flesh. When you sit on his lumpy couch and eat bowls of gross canned soup, it's physically painful not to be touching him. You want his body near yours at all times. You remember faintly that he's supposed to have kids but don't ask him about them.

Zack tells you he's never felt this way, not even with any of his wives. Zack tells you he's going to get his act together, sober up, get a job. Be worthy of you. Sometimes Zack cries quietly into your neck. Holding him in these moments feels like what your body is meant to do.

"Sssshh," you say, like you're wise. "It's all going to be okay."

One night neither of you have money left to taxi out to a new club, so Zack says he'll drive.

"We don't have to party hard tonight, babe. We can just go and dance."

A distant warning bell chimes in your head, but Zack's electric kiss mutes it.

For an hour Zack is true to his word, but then somehow you both decide drinking is okay as long as Zack stays away from cocaine and ecstasy. By midnight you're stumbling drunkenly into his car. By twelve-thirty you've crashed into another vehicle and the police are on their way.

"Shit, baby," Zack says, banging his hands against the steering wheel.

You turn your neck to see if it is hurt. You both get out of the car at the same time as the other couple. They are tourists, with their fanny packs and their "I Heart Hollywood" T-shirts. They are your parents' age and look dazed and frightened. Their car is smashed, but they seem to be walking okay. Shame awakens inside you. Zack's red flags resurface, blazing through your mind.

"Babe, if I get one more strike, I'm going to jail for a long time," he says, tugging your arm. "Please say you were driving. Please."

The wailing police car draws closer. You and Zack stand

frozen in the glare of the headlights. You're still half-drunk, disheveled, and sick to your stomach. You're not a bad girl, like sexy. You're a bad girl, like a horrible degenerate. You could have killed those innocent people. You could have died. Suddenly, you miss flossing.

"Please, baby," Zack repeats. "I love you. I love you so much it scares me."

If you want to cover for your beloved criminal, turn to page 169, section 46.

If it's time to start living responsibly, turn to page 35, section 12.

46

French philosopher Blaise Pascal once wrote, "The heart has reasons that reason knows not."

So you're sure at least he would understand when you say, "Officer, I was the one driving the car. I'm so sorry."

For some odd reason Officer Ruiz doesn't really care that you're sorry. He must not read a lot of romantic poetry. And he's not buying your little doe-eyed routine. You are not legally permitted to drive Zack's car. And the blood-alcohol-concentration test gives you a score of .077, just below the criminal level of .08. Ruiz thinks it's close enough and gives you a ticket to appear in court. He tells you your license will be suspended, you'll pay a huge fine, and you will need to do community service.

"Or you could plead not guilty and go to trial," he continues in a monotone. He has a ring on his finger and likely wants to go home to his wife.

You have no idea what he's talking about—words like "trial" and "community service" are for hardened criminals, not for a foolish girl in love!

You're so nervous you're shaking, but Zack's look of gratitude melts you.

By the time you get back to his place you've forgotten all

about the ticket, which is crumpled in your back pocket.

You will miss your court date, which is a misdemeanor.

You will miss the letter telling you about said misdemeanor and what steps you must take to address it, including a $6,000 fine.

You will be holed up with Zack, enjoying another debauched afternoon—both of you weeping with unbridled codependence—when the knock will come on the door.

As Officer Ruiz drags your butt to jail, Zack promises he'll visit, but you suspect differently.

THE END

47

It would be shallow to go with that cocky-looking architect just because he claims to be rich. That's not what you're about! You're about . . . wait, what are you about? Gentle Smile will be here in ten minutes, and you want to have a firm sense of what you're looking for this time. After sweeping on some eyeliner and smoothing your first-date jeans, you jot down a quick list:

What I'm About:

Kindness.

Humor.

Commitment.

Shared interests and go—

The doorbell rings and whoa! He is much more handsome in person than he was in his photo! You remember another important quality for your list: *hotness.* Jun is half-Japanese and strapping with a regal nose, thick arched brows, and a mop of silky black hair. He looks like a nonchalant prince. Holy crap, why would this guy like yo—

"Wow, you're much prettier in real life," he says, and his smile in person is downright dazzling. Uh-oh, maybe you should have worn something else!

The glitter in Jun's black eyes suggests that maybe he doesn't mind. He looks around your cluttered apartment and says it's charming. He takes your hand and says, "I hope you like Cuban food."

You don't mention that you like almost all food nor that the touch of his strong hand sends your heart fluttering. To your surprise, Jun doesn't lead you to his car but rather on a short stroll to a nearby Cuban café that you adore. Very few people even know about this little hideaway. Is Jun amazing or what?

Calm down—being handsome and knowing about a restaurant does not make him a god. Getting instantly swept off your feet is immature, remember? You determine to really get to know him and think up exposing questions to ask him like, "What is your biggest fear?" and "Do you follow your ex-girlfriends on Twitter?"

Then a strange thing happens over shredded flank steak simmered in cumin over saffron rice. Jun manages to sidestep all your questions and keep the attention focused completely on you. He is the most attentive listener you have ever met in the male form. He asks you what you're reading, what you eat for breakfast, and he laughs uproariously at the crazy story about your mom's appendicitis. Normally you love ropa vieja, but you're chattering so much that you barely touch your plate!

You blush, afraid you've been monopolizing the conversation. Jun's casual but sexy demeanor makes you feel feverish.

"Jesus, I've been babbling forever," you say, looking down at your sautéed onions.

"And it's utterly charming," he says, gently nudging your chin up so you can meet his gaze.

That's the second time he's used the word "charming," which is in itself charming. Your heart squeezes inside its little chamber.

"Well, tell me about you—I mean, where do you live?" you ask.

"Oh, not too far," he says, then, "wow, this cubed pork is a revelation!"

You laugh and somehow start talking about food (you're both obsessed), books (he's read a few), and politics (he's well informed).

Suddenly it's midnight. You guys have been talking for over four hours. Is it just the frozen mojitos, or are you giddy from a magical evening?

Jun walks you home and does not ask to come inside. Instead, he presses his mouth against yours for the briefest of seconds and says, "I'd love to see you again."

You repress the urge to push him against your door and run your tongue all over his teeth. *Play hard to get*, you tell yourself.

For your second date Jun picks you up in a rented Honda (his car is in the shop) and drives you to the beach to have a picnic. There is wine, homemade katsu sando sandwiches, and some dizzying kisses on the sand. He takes you back home and kisses you intensely at the door.

Date three is a funny indie movie, followed by an intimate wine bar and heavy petting in his rental car. Jun's caresses are slow and steady, like he could do this all night and never lose patience. Did you walk up the stairs to your apartment or float?

On the fourth date you get a cold and Jun actually comes over with soup and DVDs. He cuddles you and nothing more. Through the phlegm and cotton-head, your loins are on fire. Postponing sex is hotter than sex. How much longer can you wait?

By the fifth date you're back to health and offer to pick *him* up, but he refuses. He picks you up at eight and comes in to use the bathroom. There is a plan to see a local band play a concert, but you never make it out of your apartment. The clothes start flying off, and his body is so stunning, you're afraid to reveal your own. Why is his body so good? Why is his skin so luminous? Why are even his fingernails, like, perfect?

Instead of asking, you let yourself melt into his kisses and into the best sex of your life. Jun is so good, you have the crazy thought that maybe he's a male prostitute. The fact is, you're still not totally clear about what he does—like, work for his father's laundry business or something?

Your leg wraps around his waist and you gaze up at him.

"That was incredible," you whisper. You hope he hasn't noticed he has less hair than you.

"You're incredible," he says, causing you to practically swoon.

Then you say, "What do you do again?"

There's a long silence. Jun doesn't look nervous, just thoughtful. You snuggle up and inhale papaya in his neck.

"I really like you," he says.

"I really like you," you say back.

"I want to see you again this Friday."

"Sure . . . but are you avoiding my question?"

"You promise you'll see me Friday?" he insists.

"Okay!" you relent. "Maybe I can come over."

Jun is silent again. You're swimming in the black sea of his eyes when it suddenly hits you: Jun is broke. Jun is ashamed.

"You don't have a real job, do you?" you ask.

"Nope," he says, in a way that seems both noble and humble. He probably doesn't even have a car—hence the rental!

The question is, *Do you care?*

> Absolutely not. You are here to find love, not a benefactor.
> Turn to page 176, section 48.

> Kinda, maybe you shouldn't . . . but you do.
> Turn to page 194, section 52.

48

"I'd love to come over Friday," you tell Jun, and you mean it. True love is the only prosperity you're looking for, and everyone knows this economy is downright brutal.

The rest of the week you alternate from daydreaming about sleeping with Jun again to congratulating yourself for not caring about his financial status. Like you're so great for liking a gorgeous, charismatic dude who happens to be having a hard time—get over yourself! It's not like you come from money either—you come from a middle-class background, back when there was a middle class. You went to public school, and your parents often fought over electric bills and car insurance. And yet you've begun imagining yourself as a queen compared to Jun.

Bring a bathing suit! he texts you on Friday, and you picture the dinky little pool his shabby apartment building probably has.

"This pool is super!" you might say. No—too condescending.

"Great to be able to take a swim, ain't it?" No—too avuncular.

You're mulling over other options as you drive mindlessly through the winding road to Malibu. Some dilapidated beach shack awaits you—

Wait, this is weird. You're at the house.

Wait.

You're at the house, right?

The address is correct. But you check again to make sure. Yes, correct.

Jun does not live in a shack. Jun lives in a mansion. *Jun is loaded.*

"I never say it up front," he tells you, leading you into the magnificent luxury estate. "Chicks can get weird about that kind of stuff. I usually wait months, to be honest. But something about you . . ." he circles his arm around your waist and pulls you into a kiss. You feel lightheaded for a moment.

All week when Jun was poor (in your mind), you felt benevolent and in control. Now it's like he has all this status, and you're just a little dust mite. So his dad made a fortune on a well-known sitcom—why should your dynamic change so rapidly based on a TV show about a talking monkey?

"It's just money," you say, willing this to be so. Money for guys is like beauty for girls—way too much emphasis placed on it, and in the end it shouldn't matter at all.

But this doesn't mean you don't enjoy drinking daiquiris in his shimmering pool and kissing passionately in the hot tub.

And in the weeks that follow you don't exactly mind watching movies in the "screening room" or lounging at pool parties with big movie directors and bewitching actresses or having a cook whip you up berry-stuffed crêpes for a snack and a housekeeper who cleans and folds your laundry. Not to mention getting naked with Jun in every room in the place at every time of day. Jun's body is so beautiful. It's lean and smooth without looking like it's trying too hard. Every time you touch it a thrill rushes through you. No, it would be a stretch to say you mind these things.

And it wouldn't be fair to say you've *moved in* either. It's just that Jun encourages you to stay there all the time, and your hot stuffy little apartment, after all this . . . well, it would just feel wrong. Chilled water with floating cucumbers by the bed tables and soft pillows plumped daily—these things feel right.

"These pillows are dreamy," you mumble one morning, pulling Jun back into bed. His hair falls in his eyes. God, what you wouldn't give for Jun's mop of thick, silky hair!

"You're dreamy," he says and kisses your nose before jumping into the giant steam shower.

It's stirring the way Jun always flatters you, but the intelligence and attentiveness that initially drew you to him may have less depth than you thought. It might have been more about charm—that easy, entitled, dazzling charm that belongs to the super-rich. The car in the shop? A Bentley. And as to why his skin and hair and teeth are so good . . . well, you know now. Jun has the most expensive soaps and lotions in the world, and if this relationship ends, you are taking all of them.

Hold on—who said anything about ending? Jun is warm

and affectionate, plus the bed is so comfy, and the pool so refreshing . . .

You're floating in it right now, sun-drenched and tipsy as you are most days now. The sun is warm and lazy on your skin, the undulating waves of the pool lulling you into half-sleep. You can barely hear the murmurs of the others—Jun is having another little get-together. He always introduces you as his girlfriend now, which is amazing.

This is good, you think. *This is natural. This is how life ought to be.*

You flip over to maybe swim a few laps and see Jun in the hot tub, laughing with a delicate blonde with perfect features. Did he—did he just kiss her? Jun dunks his head in the water and emerges laughing. You don't even know if you saw what you think you saw. Your stomach lurches.

"Hey babe!" he calls over. "Come in!"

You opt to keep floating and don't bring it up until nighttime when everyone is gone and you can have Jun all to yourself. Dusk is your favorite part of the day. You and Jun sit outside every early evening to watch the sunset and kiss endlessly.

"Jun," you say now, breaking away from his sun-warmed mouth.

"Did you . . . did you kiss that actress today? In the hot tub?"

"Marlene?" Jun asks casually.

"I don't know her name," you say. "The blonde."

"Oh. Yeah, we hook up sometimes . . . is that a problem?" he looks genuinely concerned. You are crestfallen.

"Well . . . yes? I mean, am I your girlfriend?" You feel somehow shamefully needy and unevolved just for asking this.

"Aww, come here," he says, wrapping his arms around you and nibbling your neck.

"You know you're my number-one girl," he croons.

"But . . . so why did you kiss her?" you ask. Your stomach is cramping up.

Jun turns you around now, in that imperious way that you can't help but be attracted to. "Listen," he says intently. "I'm, like . . . I'm in love with you."

"You are?" you ask.

"Yeah . . . I used to just go online to meet more women to fuck."

"What?!"

"I'm just being honest," Jun says. Everything he says always sounds both casual and sincere. He could tell you California has been taken over by zombies and somehow convey genuine concern and total nonchalance at the same time. "Things have changed, though," he continues. "I'm getting older. I want someone to settle down with, and I have a good feeling it could be you."

"Oh my god," you whisper. Your head is spinning with

181

romantic fantasies. You and Jun drinking sangria in St. Bart's. You and Jun strolling in Paris, feeding each other pistachio macarons. You and Jun siring a noble line of children with perfect noses.

"But I'm not going to give up my lifestyle."

Thud.

Oh right. You almost forgot about the kiss. Jun isn't going to give up his lifestyle. Jun wants to settle down but also sleep with as many ingénues as he likes. It's the kind of paradox that only rich people can demand with a straight face.

But would it be so bad? Being fabulously wealthy for life, with the only price being an occasional dalliance on Jun's part? That would probably happen with most guys anyway. And here, at least, you'd still be his "number-one girl." If you had kids, you'd never have to worry about money for a second—they could go to Yale! They could be anything! You could drink all the cucumber water in the world and have the best skin and hair, just like Jun. And, of course, you'd have Jun. Beautiful, charismatic Jun.

You remember the way your mom mended your shoddy middle-school backpack all the way through twelfth grade rather than "waste money" on a new one. The way your dad yelled if you took a long shower because of the water bill. Those memories are dear to you now—who would you become if you join this strange and stirring bourgeois society? Do you want to find out?

If a life of luxury sounds peachy keen,
turn to page 184, section 49.

If you're not going to throw away your principles,
turn to page 187, section 50.

49

"Okay," you tell Jun. "I won't ask you to give up your lifestyle."

"Good," he whispers into your ear. "I love you."

You close your eyes, ashamed. That night you don't have sex with Jun, and your dreams are thick with anxiety.

But after a few weeks it's amazing how quickly you fall back into things. There are more parties, and then sailing, and then Jun takes you to wine country for a few days. The cuisine there is decadent, but you're beginning to wonder whether you need to write your food articles anymore. Who else needs to know about Osetra Caviar, veal sweetbreads, and beef pavé with caramelized shallot sauce?

Jun says you shouldn't bother, that you should let him take care of you now. Then he playfully throws a furry black box at you.

He doesn't even wait for the *yes*—after all, who would say no?

Your wedding is spectacular, of course. A "simple affair" in a Japanese zen garden with blue bell flowers sprinkled from above in a soft lavender rain. Gourmet Cuban chefs are flown in to honor your first date, and they keep the guests gorging on malanga fritters and frozen mojitos. Your dress—scalloped cream lace with a sweetheart neckline and jeweled ribbon sash—cost more than your college tuition.

Unfortunately your parents look uncomfortable the whole time, and you are surprised how few friends of your own made it to the guest list. You seem to have drifted apart from them lately, even Crystal. It's like they don't understand you anymore or something.

Luckily Jun does. Or at least he's good at pretending to. You start learning that charm is different from warmth. At dinner Jun flashes his dazzling smile, then goes back to his phone. And soon he gets wrapped up in other things: pilot lessons, art collecting, scuba diving. Jun throws himself into each project with the passion he showed you in those first few months. Then he gets restless. Being able to do whatever he wants all the time is boring for him. For you, it's paralyzing. Sometimes it takes you thirty minutes to decide what to eat for breakfast. After all, the possibilities are endless.

Perhaps that's how Jun feels about casual sex, a hobby he hasn't grown tired of. When he sneaks into bed in the middle of the night, you know where he's been. And you're not "allowed" to say anything. So you just roll over and pretend to be asleep, quickly brushing the hot tears aside and stuffing your face in the freshly plumped pillow.

The years flow by like this—shimmering, easy, and sad. You have the most exquisite clothes in the world, but who cares? You're never too hot nor too cold, but shouldn't you be? You float in the sumptuous pool every day. You float and float, and part of you floats away. The old you, the one full of passion and curiosity, has been replaced by someone lazy, imperious, and stultified.

Get out, a voice whispers to you. *Get out while you can still make a new life for yourself. A life of your own.*

But then comes the fresh-squeezed orange juice and warm, fluffy croissants on a silver tray. Then come weekly deep-tissue massages, a second home in London, and organic shampoo infused with Hawaiian honeysuckle. It's the only shampoo that has ever made your frizzy hair look good. *Ever.* You have a queasy feeling you'll be lathering with it for years to come . . .

THE END

50

For a split second you consider letting Jun whisk you away into a life of luxury, but then you come to your senses. First of all, people who are too rich get weird. Second of all, as painful as it is to admit . . . Jun is a giant d-bag.

You tell him you just can't sign up to this life, stuff some expensive lotion into your bag, and get out of there. Soon you're back to your old world of food blogging, reading classics on your old lumpy couch, and cocktails with Crystal.

But late at night, lying on your back in your plain old bed, it bothers you that you were so tempted by Jun's offer. You wouldn't have thought yourself so susceptible to the lure of money. You want to know more. So you head to one of the last remaining bookstores in town and find yourself in the nonfiction section, leafing through a book called *Affluenza*.

"Ooh, that's a good one," says a scruffy-looking guy you hadn't noticed before. He wears funky glasses, cargo pants, and a big afro. His face is playful and beatific—a cross between your childhood swim teacher and black Jesus. It works.

"Oh, is it?" you ask.

"Yeah, I've read it several times." He's got a backpack on one shoulder and holds a thick book about corporate fat cats.

"I'm Amad," he says.

"I'm—"

"Quite beautiful," he interrupts.

By nightfall you guys are eating pepperoni pizza at a hole-in-the-wall joint in Echo Park. You always were a sucker for compliments. And unlike Jun, Amad is short on cash but long on substance. Talking with him doesn't make you feel dizzy like Jun did, but you're compelled by everything he says. Maybe that's what it means to like someone in a mature way?

"So why were you reading that fat-cat book?" you ask him.

"I'm a Marxist," he says warmly. "Unfettered capitalism is ruining our country."

"Oh," you say, remembering Jun's steam shower and cucumber water. "I see what you mean."

"But we don't need to get into it. I'm not a proselytizer or anything. Tell me more about you!"

Normally you'd be happy to oblige, but you're too darn curious about *him*. You've been leading such a shallow, navel-gazing life with Jun—you're suddenly thirsty for cheap beer and new ideas with Amad!

You start spending lots of time together. Amad knows everything about global politics, racism, and economics, and he has traveled all over the world. Not sight-seeing like Jun but instead digging ditches and helping people in poor countries get clean water. He's the real deal—a good person who actually does good work. Being with him feels like it elevates you too. Let's face it: the only money you've ever given to charity is leftover saag paneer to the homeless guy outside your favorite Indian restaurant. And only when you're really full. Amad has actually been to India to, like, help.

He's also a generous lover, believing that women have been objectified in the same way workers have and that their bodies should be honored, not reduced to degraded meat on billboards and in music videos. He expresses this honoring through studious attention to all your body parts. Marxism is beginning to look pretty good.

And Amad is growing cooler by the minute. When you think about Greg and Jun, you realize that charm actually predicts bad outcomes. Charm has nothing to do with someone's ability to be a good partner. Amad is a wonderful partner. He's caring, kind, and always considerate of your feelings. You decide to attend a political meeting with him to show him that *you* care. Amad is elated.

When the big night comes, you get jittery, picturing a dark cellar full of angry bespectacled mobs burning money. In reality, it's just some young woman's apartment where normal people eat cold pizza and argue over the best way to get their newsletter out—like should they use Twitter or not. It reminds you of being on the high school paper. It's fun.

Back home that night you're wiping tomato sauce off Amad's T-shirt when suddenly you both blurt something out at the same time.

You blurt: "I love you."

He blurts: "Move to Haiti with me."

Then in unison, both of you: "What?"

"You first," Amad says, kissing you softly.

"I think I love you," you say again.

"And I am bat-shit crazy in love with you," he says in his earnest, endearing way. "Move to Haiti with me," he says, taking your hand and placing it against his ebony cheek. "I know it sounds crazy, but there's so much suffering going on over there. I know we haven't known each other that long, but I will totally commit myself to making you happy. I won't get lost in the mission. I just think nothing could be better than making the world a better place with the most lovely woman I've ever met."

You look into Amad's eyes and believe every word—believe in his love, believe that he's leading a worthwhile life, believe that you could be part of it.

You also believe that Haiti is really far away. With desperation. And poverty. And no cable television. Leaving Jun's palace was one thing, but are you ready to take it to the next level?

If you're ready to travel coach to Haiti with a wonderful man,

turn to page 192, section 51.

If jumping from one extreme to another doesn't feel right,

turn to page 133, section 37.

51

Being with Amad has awakened something inside you—an interest in the world outside yourself. It's outrageous how much energy you have spent in the pursuit of something as trivial as *finding a guy*. It's embarrassing. Going to Port-au-Prince—attempting to be of service, even if it's just sweeping the beach one grain at a time—that sounds worthwhile.

But it turns out life in Haiti is very tough. For six months you live in a flimsy tent in Titanyen, north of Port-au-Prince. You spend hours all day doing backbreaking physical labor, helping to build houses. It's sort of awful. Your bum knee swells up on a daily basis, you'd kill for a ten-minute shower, and there is a widespread problem of defecating on streets. People constantly beg for money. You remember Jun's pool and feel sick to your stomach.

"Yeah, of course it's bad," Amad says one night on your little cot. "That's why we're here."

You sigh and snuggle up to him, even though you're both sweaty and gross. You used to think you were a good person, but you're probably not. Amad is a good person. You're just trying.

"Trying to be good is a form of goodness," Amad says and smoothes your hair.

Jesus, maybe he really is Jesus.

You look at him one evening over *diri kolé ak pwa* (rice and beans). His face is luminous as he pores over a book. Amad is the dearest man you've ever known. As he teaches you about environmental racism and sustainable construction, you teach him how to lighten up. There's no way to be an aid worker in Haiti without some laughs. As in all subjects, Amad is a quick study, and his goofy side begins to emerge.

Little by little he teaches you how to be good. You are able to move on from physical labor and into an organization that works to improve women's literacy and job opportunity. And here you find your true vocation. All that fitful energy you had all those years, energy that you projected onto one dingbat dude after another, now has a meaningful place to focus.

It's not like you'll do a world of good. In the nonprofit world a tiny, tiny difference is all you're gonna get. But it feels like something you're good at, something that matters. And coming back to your tent to see Amad's shining face? Well, that's just icing on the cake.

And it's delicious.

THE END

52

No one would ever accuse you of being very successful. But you manage to keep your head above water, pay for health insurance, and keep up enough income to drive a working car. You'd like a guy who can do the same—is that so unfair?

You let Jun off the hook in the same way many men have dumped you—by flaking on plans, only returning some phone calls, and slowly sort of dropping off. Dating is a brutal business; it's kill or be killed. One minute, game on; the next minute, game off. It's not at all what your mother told you dating would be like—with flowers at the door and kisses on your hand. You decide to go offline for a while and just concentrate on living a fuller life. After all, people always say that's when you're more likely to meet someone. Those people are probably lying, but it's worth a shot.

You refocus on your career and start going to more restaurants, writing more, and brainstorming different formats for your food criticism—like a web show or a documentary. The renewed focus on your career lifts your spirits immensely. At Crystal's insistence you even start tweeting little bon mots about food. You always said you'd never tweet, but at a certain point you gotta join the party.

It's strange how that forges relationships with total strangers. One follower named J. P. often retweets your tweets. So you follow him and find that he mostly posts links to obscure art openings or *New York Times* book reviews. You start retweeting *his* tweets, even when you don't read the articles.

This finally results in J. P. asking you out. And some people might call a minigolf date stupid, but you think it's fun! And maybe he's not built like Jun or cocky like Greg, but he's definitely got *something*.

Something you want to know more about. Something that has you tossing and turning in your sleep, biting your pillow with excitement. You want to keep seeing him.

Get out there and explore, Lady Magellan!
Turn to page 87, section 26.

53

You leave Max a plain note: *I just can't trust you anymore.*

Then you start packing your bags. There will be time for divorce papers and visitation rights later, but for now you just want to get out of here.

As you stuff your clothes and soaps in an old suitcase, your mind races. *How did you get here? Whose fault is it? Do all men cheat? When will this pain go away? What is the purpose of life?*

You remember what you learned in Artie's Mommy and Me yoga class: breathe. You stop your manic packing and sit down for a minute. You simply sit with your breath and watch your thoughts, the way they range from fury to self-hatred to grim determination to a sort of nothingness and then back again. You send your exhale right into your heart, which feels like a volcano. It's so hot inside you, you're desperate to bolt, but you keep sitting for another minute. You sit with the sizzling pain in your guts. You let your shoulders release.

And a strange kind of calm comes over you. The nightmare—your husband cheating on you with a young beautiful woman—has happened. That's it. It happened, and you're alive. You're in agony, but you're alive. There's a certain freedom that comes from that. And sitting at the foot of your and Max's bed, watching your breath, has stirred something in you. A wish for something even more elusive than a partner: a sense of inner peace.

It's not long before you find a Buddhist monastery tucked in a wooded region in Southern California. They need help cleaning, washing, gardening, and cooking. Simple tasks to reunite you with simple needs. No television. No Facebook. No microwave chicken nuggets. Artie is welcome there. In the mornings you chant; in the evenings you meditate silently. Daytime is for chores, reading to Artie, studying ancient texts, and hiking through the back trails of the mountain. Sitting on a tree stump under the glimmering sun, it all seems so clear. The way you've grasped desperately at a security that simply doesn't exist in this lifetime. What a relief it would be if you could learn to unclench those hands.

You never dreamed you'd end up a Buddhist monk. But life, as you are learning, is an adventure and an experiment. It's not about being married or single, living in a house or on a commune. You seek peaceful unity with all living things. It's a task so mysterious and profound, it could take a lifetime.

THE END

54

You will allow this handsome stranger to drive you home, but you're not foolish enough to believe he is your soul mate.

For one thing, he's far too hot. You're uncomfortable even being in the car with him. His chest is practically ripping through his T-shirt. His golden calves burst forth from his ratty army-cargo shorts. He's so tall and hulky, you wonder how he fits in his own car. It's hard to even think of him as a person; instead, you keep thinking of him as "the body." As in, *I'm so close to the body in this car*, or *What would happen if I touched the body?* It's unfortunate that you are so distracted because he's actually making great conversation.

When he pulls up to your apartment, you figure it would be stupid to leave without at least hugging the body. Instead, you lean over and do the weird thing you've been dying to do the whole ride home: you lick him. You lick his face, his neck, and you yank his shirt up and lick his glorious broad chest.

"Are you a little puppy?" he asks, laughing huskily but not stopping you.

"Arf!" you bark. "Arf! Arf!" Midbark, you kiss him with every bit of passion roiling inside you. You kiss him and kiss him and kiss him until you can't breathe.

Then you leap out of his car, purple with embarrassment.

Fine, so you just pretended to be a dog to get some action. Over and done with. Back to your life. But now your life is absolutely unacceptable. Licking a man like a pathological puppy has freed you. It's time to stop complaining about the land of silicone and agave syrup and get out of here!

You call your favorite magazine editor and demand she let you do a travel tour of European street foods. Normally such a thing would be unheard of, but the gods have suddenly taken a turn in your favor. You set off on an international adventure.

Soon you are traveling around Europe and wrapped up in your other passion: food. You eat during the day and pore over your computer at night. Focusing on your work buoys your confidence again. Who else but you should be commenting on the fluffy intimacy of a Parisian croissant or the casual elegance of a mushroom and truffle focaccia in Barcelona? What if you put together a book about it . . . or a documentary . . . or wrote a song?

Okay, maybe not a song, but the point is your creative juices are flowing. It's fun not to think about men and to think about your own potential for a change. Plus, you're stimulated by the gorgeous sound of other languages, the fun of befriending other English speakers, going to ancient ruins and discotheques—you are a true adventurer!

You're congratulating yourself for being amazing as you gobble up some pastitsio at a charming Greek café. You've really turned it around, haven't you? You're resilient—like Greece. You feel a connection with this country, which has seen such hard times but manages to retain such warmth and friendliness. You're so wrapped up in your thoughts, you almost don't notice the waiter who brings you a glass of ouzo. But the hand holding the check is bronze and strong. And when you look up, well, you'd have to be in a coma not to notice that he is a veritable Greek God. The thick brows, the high cheekbones, the sinewy body. The hunk makes tire-guy seem downright homely!

Cool your jets, lusty lady.
Turn to page 83, section 24.

Greece is a paradise—enjoy it!
Turn to page 46, section 15.

55

You can't kid yourself that you love Greg anymore. The fact is, you love J. P. and you blew it. You tell Greg the timing is wrong and let him slither home. Now you're alone in the quiet to survey the wreckage.

Everything has been thrown off track. Right now J. P. and you should be moving in together. You would take a trip to Office Depot where you would get bored and bratty and he would know just what to buy, and afterward you'd go eat grilled cheese sandwiches at your favorite diner, and when you got home he'd surprise you with a beautiful teapot for your new place.

You'd settle into living together, and J. P. would Netflix all these important foreign films but you'd always say, "Let's watch *30 Rock* instead," until one day you'd agree to watch some documentary about Dick Cheney, and when you pulled out the disk, a ring would pop out, and at the wedding you'd have an awesome cover band and marzipan cake, and then you'd have two kids, one natural and one adopted from a Hungarian orphanage, and J. P. would make you go to tiny art galleries with lewd exhibitions but would also chaperone the eighth-grade dance, and when your kids went to college, you'd both write a book together about how to keep the sex alive in a marriage after twenty years, and when you got old he wouldn't care about all your wrinkles and weird little cysts forming under your eyes, and then when he was a hundred and you were ninety-four, you'd die in your sleep, holding hands, and the last thing he'd ever say was, *I love you so much, honey. I'm so glad I never left you just 'cause you kissed my brother.*

You dream of this every night. Sure, you knuckle down, concentrate on your work, and manage to eat your vegetables. But mostly you just have this dream of J. P. After all, there's a chance it could happen. And then, after four difficult months, you get the knock on the door. The special five-knock-plus-one that is J. P.'s signature.

In the movies you'd open the door and rush right into his open arms, where you'd find sweet forgiveness followed by immediate elopement.

But this is real life, so what happens is J. P. is angry and confused but still half in love with you and doesn't know what to do. There might be some couples counseling with an itchy couch and a sliding scale followed by the rebuilding of trust and a deeper, more mature intimacy.

Or maybe J. P. will fall in love with the therapist, and you'll be on your own for a decade and eventually meet a devoted divorcee with two mopey kids.

Or maybe you'll be single forever but at relative peace with that.

At the moment, standing at the doorway with your heart pounding, it's simply uncertain, which is all life and love ever promised to be. This is a painful fact, and it's the reason you never *could* be a girl like Oasis. It's the reason love can be every bit a dreadful, terrifying chore as much as the gorgeous glowing thing we all ache for until the end.

THE END

ACKNOWLEDGMENTS

Thank you…

For love and support: my amazing family and husband.

For endless listening and idea-bouncing: Nick Cain, Lucy (unicorn) Rimalower, Maggie Rowe, Debra Freeman, Chris Dewan, Rob Walz, Andy Gersick, Via Strong, India Donaldson, Natasha Parnell, Matt Price, Leila Gerstein, and Avi Glazer.

For hands-on help: Maggie Rowe, Lisa Medway, and Caryn Greenberg.

For generosity and guidance: Rina Mimoun, Gitti Daneshvari, Matthew Pearl, and Jen Besser.

For rock-star teamwork and expertise: Jason Richman, Allison Hunter, Jordana Tusman, Joshua McDonnell, Jacob Thomas, Carolyn Sobczak, Josephine Mariea, Running Press, and Perseus Books Group.